I0533110

Erotic Verses

—ɷ—

A collection of erotic poems and short stories Vol. I.5

"Winner of the 2014 Dayton Book Expo Best Selling Fiction Award"

By
P D Baldwin

ISBN: 0615869246
ISBN-13: 9780615869247

Contents:

Acknowledgements

First of all, let me begin by saying that it was never my intention to write this book. I decided to write it as a means of pushing my own creative limits while still managing to tell a great story. I wanted to test my ability to engage all the senses at once without reinventing the wheel. *Erotic Verses* is a fresh perspective; my perspective and I want to share it with you.

The whole idea came about after a series of thoughts, conversations, and questions that my peers were sharing. Basically, we got together and discussed something we all love very much; sex! Don't judge me for saying that because if it weren't for sex, we wouldn't be here, unless of course, you were hatched or something like that. *Erotic Verses* is not only about exploring sex. It's about exploring great sex! It's not meant to be an instructional manual or the new bible of sex. Erotic Verses is about expression, freedom, and unadulterated pleasure. So many men and women don't enjoy sex because they live in a box. They're afraid to share their inner most desires and fantasies for fear of being labeled as "nasty", "freaky", or some other term that sexually repressed individuals like to use. I say so what? You only live once, so why not make the best of it?

Now I'm not advocating promiscuity or just sharing your desires with anyone who comes along because such behavior will take away from that special moment. But there is absolutely nothing wrong with exploring them with a lover, spouse, or significant other. In fact, I encourage you to share this book with them. And once you do, watch out because you may discover a side of them that you never knew existed. So, enjoy!

As with anything in life, *Erotic Verses* is not intended for all audiences. The stories contained within are fictitious accounts that some will regard as vulgar, sexist, tasteless, perverted, demeaning, and a whole bunch of other words and phrases which are used to cast a shadow of negativity on an otherwise beautiful thing. To them I say, thank you for reading. After all, how would you know if you hadn't? To the rest of you who aren't afraid to explore your wild side and who refuse to be sexually repressed, I say, fasten your seatbelts and enjoy the ride.

Finally, no list of acknowledgements is complete without actually acknowledging someone. First and foremost, I'd like to thank the Most High God for the talent, and the courage, and for surrounding me with a circle or supporters and well-wishers who have pushed and motivated me. It's people like you that make this fun. And last, but certainly not least, I'd like to thank the doubters, and non-believers because whether you believe it or not, you have inspired me too.
Sincerely

P. D. Baldwin

P.S. Check me out at www.darkhalfproductions.com and on Facebook at
Dark Half Productions@facebook.com for a list of upcoming projects and their release dates.

To all my friends, fans, and family I sincerely thank you for making Erotic Verses winner of the 2014 Dayton Book Expo Best Selling Fiction Award! I couldn't have done it without you!

Phone Sex

"Hey, baby," she cooed seductively after picking up her phone.

"Hello, sexy," he replied. "I'm sorry I had to leave before I could see you one last time. I miss you already. I especially miss watching you apply lotion to that sexy body of yours."

"I miss you too," she said while sitting on the edge of the bed and caressing her soft skin with cocoa butter. "But, such is the life of an up-and-coming future CEO."

"I left you a present."

"I noticed," she said while looking at the large, pink gift box with its red satin ribbon. "It said 'Don't open until later.' So needless to say, I've been anxiously waiting for you to call."

"Now's as good a time as any to open it, but can you do me a favor first?"

"What's that?" she asked while eagerly tugging at the box's lid.

"Go over to the stereo and press *play*."

"Okay, baby."

She climbed off the California king and walked over the cherry bureau at the foot of the bed. After opening the double doors, she turned the power on and pressed *play*. The sensual sounds of horns, piano, and bass guitar filled the quiet room. As if hypnotized by the rhythm, her curvaceous hips began to sway back and forth.

"I love it!" she declared when she picked the phone up.

"Splendid. Now, do me another favor. Put the phone on speaker and lay it on the bed next to you."

"What are you up to, Mr. Sexy Man?"

"How can I be up to anything?" he asked half laughing. "I'm over a thousand miles away. Now, open your gift."

"Oh, so forceful; you know I like that shit," she cooed while lifting the pink and red lid off the box.

With a smile on her face, she surveyed its contents: a bottle of chocolate syrup, a pair of scented candles and a small torch to light them with, and something wrapped in a black scarf.

"What in the world is all this for? A dildo, seriously?" she asked after removing the silk wrap.

"Yes, darling. I made you a 'when-I'm-away-from-home kit' to keep you company on those cold, lonely nights. What do you think?"

"I think you had too much time on your hands baby," she replied with hints of sarcasm in her sexy tone. "I haven't used a vibrator since college. And exactly what am I going to do with the chocolate sauce?"

"Just relax and play along. I'll show you. Trust me, it'll be fun," he mused. "Now tell me, what do you have on that delectable body of yours?"

"Well," she began, while inhaling the aroma of the French vanilla-scented candles, "I'm wearing the black nightgown that you bought for my birthday."

"You mean the lace one with the spaghetti straps?" he asked in a low, smooth tone.

"Yes baby, that one."

"Nice. Now, I need you to do me another favor."

"You and your favors," she mused. "What's next, Mr. Man?"

"I want you to turn off the lights, light the candles, and place one on either side of the bed."

"Why, baby? What's the point of all this if you're not here with me? With the exception of the dildo, these are the kinds of things we should use when you're at home, not when I'm alone."

"Well, sexy, since I'm away, we'll have to pretend that I'm there with you. Now, light the candles. They're your favorite."

"I know," she replied while admiring the flickering flames. "Okay, the candles are lit, and the lights are off. Now what would you like me to do next?"

"I want you to lie back on the pillows and breathe in and out, nice and slow. Then, I want you to lower the straps on your gown one at a time and let the girls out to play. Pretend I'm there with you."

"Um, baby, I…"

"Just do it," he interrupted in a firm, spine-tingling tone. "It'll be fun; I promise."

"Okay, done. Now what would you like me to do?"

"I want you to close your eyes and begin caressing and squeezing those big, beautiful tits of yours, and not like you're putting lotion on them either. I want you to caress them like I would if I were standing behind you. Pretend your hands are mine."

"Okay," she replied before closing her eyes and complying with his naughty request.

"Now, imagine me standing right behind you, kissing you on the shoulder and neck as I squeeze your tits and play with your nipples between my fingers. Can you feel my dick pressed against your ass?"

"Yes," she replied softly, her mind and body falling under his hypnotic spell.

His tone had her sugar walls quivering with anticipation. Though she was no stranger to sleeping nude or masturbation, she suddenly felt very vulnerable. The mood he set had taken her from her comfort zone, and even though she was alone, she felt like she had been placed on display. His soothing voice combined with the vivid pictures he was painting caused the tingle to travel directly to her G-spot. Her clit pulsated and throbbed while her hands traced the same path his hands had traveled on numerous occasions.

"Now, I want you to slide your fingers between your creamy thighs and begin stroking your clit. Circle and tease it just like I would. Play with it until your pussy is nice and wet before sliding your fingers in and out, one at a time."

"My pussy is already wet," she gasped as her eyes rolled back up into her head.

She could feel his hands; one squeezing her tits while the other teased her clit. The sensation of her fingers invading her pussy set her body ablaze. The euphoria quickly became intoxicating.

"I want you so bad!"

"Be patient, baby. Now, I want you take the dildo in your hands like it's my dick. I want you to lick and suck it like you would me. Don't worry about your OCD. I cleaned it just for you."

"You want me to give a dildo a blow job? Where's the fun in that? Besides, it's made of latex and I hate that taste in my mouth."

"That's what the chocolate sauce is for, babe. Now, pick it up."

Again, after a brief moment of hesitation, she complied. She carefully studied the caramel-colored dildo. Its contours and ridges felt exactly like his dick did when she gripped it in her hand. Even the bulging veins and swollen head were almost identical.

"What are you doing now?" he whispered with hints of anxiety in his tone.

"I'm playing with this thing. What are you doing?"

"I'm lying in bed stroking my dick while staring at pictures of you."

"Really?" she asked before her pussy instantly flooded with hot juices.

"Absolutely," he replied before releasing a sigh of pure ecstasy that sent chills up her spine.

"Damn, baby," she gasped. "Okay, I'll play along."

She quickly grabbed the bottle and popped its top. As if it were his erect dick, she held the dildo in one hand while dripping the chocolate syrup on the head. For a brief moment, she forgot about the white satin comforter underneath her. The slow cascade of the thick sauce made her mouth water. Images of his cum slowly inching towards her hand had her hypnotized.

"You're not sucking," he whispered, throwing her even deeper into this magical trance.
"Mmmmmm," she cooed after taking it deep into her mouth, savoring the sweet sauce as she slid his dick back and forth, in and out.

His grunts and moans were so erotic. The sweet sounds of his pleasure fueled her raging inferno. Once again, her imagination took over and threw her deeper and deeper into the moment. Her lover's chocolate-covered dick was sliding in and out of her tightly puckered mouth, while her tongue circled and teased his head. She imagined him shuddering when she lightly grazed it with her front teeth. The string of saliva connecting her lips to the head was like his pre-cum that she enjoyed playing with so much. The mixture of chocolate sauce and warm saliva dripping from the sides of her mouth and onto her tits made hot cum pool beneath her round ass.

"Yes, baby, suck it. Make sure my dick is nice and clean."

His commands were sending her body into overload. His moans and heavy breathing let her know that she had his undivided attention. She made sure to hold the phone closer so that he could hear her sucking and slurping loud and clear. She repeatedly deep-throated his dick before occasionally grunting and exhaling when she triggered her gag reflex.

"I want your dick inside me!" she surrendered.
"Yes baby, yes!" he moaned. "Slide me deep inside your hot wet pussy!"
"Oh…my…gawd!" she cried when she felt the dick's head graze her swollen clit before sliding past her quivering lips. "That's it, baby work that dick nice and slow for momma."

Her pussy was a raging inferno of anticipation and pulsating desire! Even though it was her hand in control, she imagined being with her lover and his big, throbbing dick pleasuring her hot, wet pussy. Each thrust was as deep and intense as his. Each vein, contour, and ridge pressed against her tightly clinched sugar walls threatening to make her pussy erupt with hot, creamy pleasure.

"Oh shit, baby, you feel so damn good!" she cried before climax after climax erupted deep from within her abdomen.

She tried to hold it back but couldn't. Though she had masturbated before, it was nothing like this! This surpassed even her wildest dreams. The heat from her juices flowing so freely across her fingers was adding to her dizzying sensations. She was physically and emotionally entrenched in this moment. The fact that he was miles away was irrelevant. The scene that he had created was so intense that she could have sworn he was in the room with her. The ambiance of her surroundings combined with the sounds of his voice was electrifying. As far as her body was concerned, he was right there feeding her inch after inch of throbbing dick. She was on fire!

"Oh...my...gawd!"
"Yes, baby, cum for me!" he demanded, his voice echoing throughout the room and sending chills throughout her quivering, sweat-covered body. "Oh...shit...damn!"
"Did you cum, baby?" she cooed while holding the dildo in one hand and caressing her erect nipples with the other.
"Oh, hell yes," he replied enthusiastically while breathing heavy sighs of relief.
"Thank you for making my night, baby," she mused in a sultry tone as her body prepared for its eminent slumber.
"Good night, sexy," he whispered before disconnecting the call.

Shortly after she had settled in and was on the verge of a peaceful slumber, she felt the covers being slowly pulled back. Warm caresses and soft kisses began teasing her ankle before slowly moving up her leg, then her thigh, then up her stomach, and finally to her bare, tingling breasts. His kiss was electrifying, sending pulses through her body that she never dreamed were possible. He had set her body ablaze with passion and desire that left her thighs quivering. He had reminded her that exploration and imagination are truly the best forms of foreplay. And just when it seemed that the journey had ended and she would be left with nothing more than memories, he was here in the flesh, ready to take her mind and body on another sensual escapade.

"I'm glad you came back to play," she cooed as he kissed and sucked her rock hard nipples.
"Show me what you learned," he whispered before kissing her soft, puckered lips.

Tobey and Carmen:

The Untold Story

From the upcoming book *Operation Cover-Up: Rise of the Black Mamba*
By P D Baldwin

A short while later, Agent Tobey Shavers who was armed with a pocket full of cash, found his way to a gentlemen's club known as *'The Velvet Rope'*. After paying a cover charge and walking down a flight-of-stairs, he entered the showroom. The thumping bass and the soundtrack's seductive lyrics made the half-naked dancers gyrate like porno stars. Feeling the rhythm himself, Shaver's bobbed his head, mostly off beat, while making his way to the stage and taking a seat. The seductive bounce of juicy asses and soft, naked tits gave his hand a mind of its own. Before he could blink, it was in and out of his pocket with a fist full of cash. The sight of his money and the liberal way he was tossing it out attracted the attention of every dancer on the stage, as well as the attention of a few jealous fellow patrons. One caramel-colored vixen with blond shoulder-length micro braids and a voluptuous frame was particularly smitten by Tobey, and slowly made her way to where he was sitting. When she saw the look on his face, she knew she had his full, undivided attention. After dropping slowly to all fours, she began a slow and deliberate cat-crawl towards him. Her feline grace and sensuality coupled with her smooth skin and curvaceous body quickly stole the show. Even the DJ voiced his own approval with a resounding "Got-Damn!"

Tobey's mouth dropped when she reached him and stood back up. He was convinced that he was staring up at the sexiest, most beautiful dancer ever created. Then suddenly, she turned around, bent over, and smiled at him from between her spread legs. The sight of her smiling face left him with shaking hands and a throbbing dick. Beads of sweat formed on his brow when she dropped slowly into a split, with her round tattooed ass stopping inches his face. His hand shivered and shook uncontrollably when he tried to place a crisp bill inside her silver G-string.

"It don't bite, baby. You can touch it," she said while looking back at her jiggling ass and his reddened face.
"What's your name?" he managed after three attempts to swallow the huge lump in his throat.
"You can call me Car'mel Delight. What's your name?"
"Tobey...Tobias Shavers," he replied meekly.
"Well Tobey, do you like what you see?"
"Yes," he replied while squirming in his seat.
"You wanna to go to the VIP?"
"Yes," he cooed while staring at, and being hypnotized by, her bodacious ass.
"Have a seat on the couch, baby," she said moments later after closing the door behind them.

The room was typical strip club affair but with an upscale, pornographic flair to it. There were dimly lit recessed lights in the walls and multicolored track lights on the ceiling. There was also a tripod-mounted video camera inside a glass case for those willing to pay for evidence of their experience, among other things.

"What goes on back here?" Tobey asked nervously while sitting on the large, burgundy sectional and watching his voluptuous vixen select some music.

"Are you serious? This is the VIP. Anything you're willing to pay for goes on back here."

"Really?"

"Yes, really," she replied after seeing his eyes nearly pop out of his head. "But let me tell you up front. I'm not a hooker or a whore. I don't fuck or suck. I dance. Is that clear?"

"Um…sure," he replied nervously. "How much does a trip to the VIP cost?"

"Well, three songs at 250 bucks a pop is 750 bucks. For that, you get the lap dance of your life. You've never been to a strip club before, have you, Tobey?" Car'mel Delight asked when she climbed onto his lap and started to grind.

"Me? Sure…sure I have…lots…lots of times," he stammered and stuttered while staring at the pair of round, jiggling 38DDs mere inches from his nose. "Okay, I'm lying. I'm actually here on business and yes, this is my first time in a strip club."

"What kind of business?" she asked, arching her back as the rhythmic sounds coursed through her veins.

"I can't say. Black Mamba…I mean Alex…I mean my partner would kill me."

"It can't be that bad, can it?" she cooed while grabbing the back of the couch and smothering him between her breasts.

"Yes it can," he replied almost in tears. "Agency work can be especially difficult when…dammit! Alex is gonna kill me."

"No he won't. There's nobody here but you and me, daddy. Don't be shy, touch me," she said before taking his hands and placing them firmly on her tattooed ass. "So, what do you do, cutie?"

"I'm a Federal Agent here to investigate drug trafficking in the area," he surrendered.

"Are you serious?" she asked, suddenly stopping her dance routine and staring into Tobey's glassy eyes.

"Very serious."

"That is so fucking cool! I'm attending UC, double majoring in Criminal Justice and Forensic Pathology. I am also studying computer forensics as well."

"Are you kidding me? I think I love you!" he declared before hugging her close to him only to realize that his face was pressed hard against her nearly bare breasts. "Oh my, damn."

"Time's up, baby," she announced when the third song ended.

"Hey, um…would you like to get some coffee after you get off tonight? I mean, if you're interested, that is."

"I'd love to Tobey, but I have to be real with you. You'll never get what you want from a woman if you don't say it with some confidence. I just have to finish my set, and we can bounce. You can meet me by the back entrance, okay?

"Cool," he exhaled as if the weight of the world had been lifted off his shoulders.

For the next hour, Tobey watched as Car'mel Delight performed several routines including a solo that made the floor around the stage look like a crowded rock concert. As he sat there listening to the music and the various conversations taking place around him, Tobey watched the hoards of sex-crazed, two-legged vultures gathering in front of the stage. The cash they were throwing in the air rained down like confetti making his four grand look like pocket change. Even though he barely knew her, Tobey found himself getting a little jealous. The sight of these animals touching and ogling the dancers, especially his Car'mel Delight was unnerving. When the show ended, he rushed to the rear entrance as instructed and waited impatiently for his date to come down the corridor. Again, his heart pounded with anticipation as she slowly made her way towards him, stopping briefly to talk with fans, fellow dancers, and other club employees.

"Ready to go, cutie?" she asked with a huge, angelic smile on her face.

"Don't hurt him," a burly, black-clad security guard interrupted before Tobey could answer.

"Shut up, Lou," she scoffed before taking Tobey by the arm and lead-ing him away.

"What's he talking about?" Tobey asked after sizing up the pale, bald headed behemoth.

"Nothing important, hon. He assumes that all the girls here turn tricks to make a fast buck. To be honest, some of them do, but not me. I prefer to use my brain to get ahead instead of my body. You feel me?"

"I think I love you," Tobey cooed again as they strolled through the parking. "Oh shit!"

"What's wrong?"

"I forgot I didn't drive here. I caught a cab from the hotel."

"That's not a problem, cutie. My car is right over here."

"Are you shittin' me?" Tobey exclaimed when he saw the electric blue Honda Civic Si Coupe and its silver graphics on gleaming eighteen inch, chrome rims wrapped in low-profile tires.

"You like it?" she asked, giddily watching as he walked around the car admiring its custom details and mirror tint.

"I love it! What do you have under the hood?"

"Not much, I'm afraid. All I have is what came from the factory. I'd really love some more power though."

"You and me both," he whispered, once again admiring her body, even though it was concealed under an overcoat.

"I've got a friend named Tango in Denver who loves modifying cars. For next to nothing, he can add a turbo charger, modify your exhaust, and reprogram your EMS. That could easily give you an extra 100 to 150 horsepower."

"For real?"

"Oh yeah," Tobey responded, his confidence building with each pass-ing second. "Of course, we'd have to upgrade your suspension, and reinforce the synchro mesh and gearing in the tranny. Plus torque steer is going to be a monster without significant modifications, so we have to make sure that all the newfound power gets to the ground and stays there. We also need to make sure you can stop, so upgraded brakes and rotors are a must."

"Interesting," she mused while gazing at him with a smile. "You're not really an agent, are you, Tobey?"

"You got me again," he muttered with his head lowered, looking for some solace while staring at his chocolate-brown Stacey Adams. "Black…I mean Alex is the agent. I'm a computer technician, but I'm the best in the world."

"It's okay, sexy. I love men who are confident in their intelligence. Brains are sexier than brawn any day."

"Really?"

"Absolutely. Now, let's go get that cup of coffee," she replied while walking to the driver's door with his eyes fixed on her swinging hips and voluptuous ass.

Hours later after coffee, waffles, and in-depth conversations, Tobey and Carmen arrived outside his hotel. After gazing at his watch and then up at the massive marquee, Tobey looked at his sexy driver and nervously made his move.

"Would it be too forward of me to ask if you wanted to come up for a while?"

"It depends on why you're asking."

"It's just that it's late, we're both tired, and I'd hate for anything to happen to you on the way home. I mean, I know we just met, but I like you."

"That's so sweet, Tobey. But if you like me so much, why haven't you asked me for my real name?"

"What is your real name?" he asked after briefly contemplating what she had just said.

"It's Carmen, and I'd love to come up, but only if you promise not to hurt me."

"I promise," he replied before almost melting in his seat.

Moments later, they entered Tobey's luxury suite, and after a brief tour, Carmen removed her coat and laid it on the couch. In the midst of their conversation, he had forgotten that she was only wearing a bikini top and a pair of black boy shorts underneath it. He quickly sat down on the couch and placed a throw pillow in his lap, hoping to conceal the tent that had risen. His reaction to her apparel didn't go unnoticed, however.

"Since it looks like I'm staying, I'm going to grab a shower. You can join me, if you like."

Tobey's mouth dropped when her words finally registered. He was frozen in place by the time she disappeared into the bathroom. Seconds later, he heard the shower come on and watched steam billow out of the door. When her clothes sailed out and hit the floor, Tobey sprang up from the couch with his bulge on full display. If this was a dream, he was determined to enjoy every single minute of it. Moments later he was standing behind Carmen in the shower, cupping his throbbing dick while watching water cascade down her silky smooth skin. His heart pounded furiously when she bent over to lather her legs and thighs.

"Don't just stand there Tobey. Make yourself useful and wash my back for me."
"O…o…okay," he gasped.

His hands shook like Jell-O when he took the soap and the wash cloth from her. He nearly dropped the bar a dozen times while staring at her naked ass. His breathing became erratic to the point that he was panting the second he touched her back. His dick threatened to explode while he made soapy circles across her shoulders, down her spine to just above her round, delectable ass.

"Thank you, honey," she replied when she turned around and faced him with a radiant smile. "Now I'll help you."

She took washcloth and soap and began scrubbing his chest and shoulders. The lower she washed, the harder he throbbed and there was no way he could hide it.

"Move your hands so I can wash you there," she said after squatting and smiling up at him. "Hello you."

With the soapy cloth in her palm, Carmen stroked and washed his hardened dick while continuing to smile at him. Her relaxed demeanor and tender touch had Tobey ready to faint. Just as his legs were about to give way, a stream of cum shot from his dick, barely missing her hardened nipple but landing on her caramel thigh. He couldn't believe it! With a smile on her face, Carmen stood up and guided him to the front of the shower. After a few more moments of soapy scrubbing and rinsing, they took turns drying each other off before turning off the lights and climbing into bed. With her back to him and seemingly sound asleep, Tobey lay there caressing his dick while staring at her ass. The pressure from his erection was excruciating. His heart pounded while his mind raced with thoughts of touching, kissing, and caressing her naked flesh.

For the next half hour, he lay there, intermittently staring at the ceiling and the sexy naked vixen next to him. When he could no longer resist the agonizing temptation, Tobey decided to take a chance. Slowly and carefully, he slid towards Carmen until he was just inches from her. His trembling hand hovered above her shoulder for what seemed like an eternity before he finally summoned the nerve to caress her soft skin. Remembering the tales he had heard his coworkers spin about their in-the-field sexual exploits, Tobey starting placing soft kisses across Carmen's shoulder.

"What took you so long?" she asked softly when his hand gently squeezed her right breast.

Before Tobey could blink, he was flat was on his back and Carmen was perched on his lap. With his hands pinned to the mattress, she kissed and sucked his lips, ears, and neck with intensity unlike anything he had ever felt before. His throbbing dick beat furiously against her wet pulsating clit, trying its best to penetrate her silky lips. After a brief battle with an unruly condom, Tobey and his dick were ready to for duty. He squeezed and caressed Carmen's tits while she hovered above his dick. Seconds later, he was deep inside her.

"You like that, baby?" she asked while sliding up and down his throbbing pole.

"Yes, Carmen, yes," he moaned while teasing her nipples between his trembling fingers.

With his eyes rolled into the back of his head and his toes curled, Tobey fought back the urge to scream. Carmen's sugar walls gripped and milked him with each rise and fall of her juicy hips. Sitting up and arching her back, she cupped his hands in hers and squeezed them over her soft tits and rock hard nipples. Her soft moans and gentle coos sent chills up and down his spine. Emboldened by her reactions, Tobey rolled Carmen onto her back, placed her left leg onto his right shoulder, and began feeding her pussy thrust after powerful thrust.

"Damn, Tobey, you workin' this sweet black pussy!" she surrendered while digging her nails into his shoulders and listening to her pussy voice its own approval.

Carmen couldn't believe what was happening. *Was this the same the shy, nerdy guy that she had just met hours ago taking her body to the point of another orgasm?* His touch was unlike any other she had ever felt. Normally, she would have felt cheap, but this was different. She could feel genuine sincerity of his voice, his kiss, and his caress. Each movement of his body was in rhythm with hers. There was no doubt in Carmen's mind that Tobey was made just for her. Everything about him from his smooth, milky skin to his shy and timid demeanor was beautiful. Unlike other men, he looked beyond her "job," and instead, saw the real person. Though he clearly loved her body, she knew that it was her mind that he was most attracted to. This revelation not only intensified her attraction to him, it also intensified her body's reaction to everything he did. With her lips quivering and her back arched, juices flowed from between her thighs like a river.

"Shit Tobey, *shit!*" Carmen cried as he hit her G-spot again and again, as if his dick knew the path straight to it.
"Oh…my…gawd!" Tobey surrendered as a rush of cum erupted from his thrusting shaft and swollen head.
"Yes, baby, yes! Give me all that nut!"
"Oh, shit!" he cried again as wave after wave erupted like a volcano spewing hot lava into Carmen's pulsating pussy.
"That's right, baby lie down and let momma hold you," she whispered, while caressing the back of his head which was nestled between her glistening breasts.
"I hope I'm not dreaming."
"Now, Tobey, why would you say something like that?"
"Because you're the most beautiful woman I've ever seen, and if I am, I hope I never wake up."
"I'm as real as real can be, baby," she replied before kissing his lips. "I hope that's not all you have for me, Agent Shavers," Carmen cooed while gently applying pressure to his dick with her tightened walls.
"N…n…no," he stuttered.
"Good, because I want to give you all this car'mel delight all night."
"Really?"
"Yes, really," she replied with a smile, before grabbing the sides of his head and thrusting her tongue deep into his mouth.

The combination of their heated kissing and her contracting walls not only massaged his dick, but made it harder and harder by the second. Before either of them realized it, Tobey's dick was fully erect once again.

Damn, white boy! Carmen thought to herself.

Before now, she'd never entertained the notion of interracial dating because it simply went against everything she'd been taught growing up. All of that went out of the window, however, because this man had shown her genuine respect, interest, and now passion. Any thoughts of explaining how they met or what she saw in him would have to wait. This man was making her body feel things that she never knew were possible.

"Do you mind if I get behind you?" he asked timidly.

"Baby, if you're gonna keep this mojo going, I'ma need you to man up."

"What do you mean?"

"I mean," Carmen began while looking deep into his ocean blue eyes, "it's like I told you earlier. If you want something from a woman, you have to say it with confidence. Otherwise, you'll never get it."

"Really?" Tobey asked, shocked by her impassioned revelation. "I didn't think that...never mind. Okay, here goes. Turn that big, sexy caramel ass around so I can tap it from behind."

"What did you say muthafucka?" she snapped.

"I'm so sorry! I...I"

"Shh...I'm just teasing, sexy," Carmen interrupted while holding him tightly. "That was good, though. A little more work and you'll be thugged out in no time. But right now, get behind this ass and command this pussy, Agent Shavers."

"Hell, yeah!" he replied feverishly.

Moments later, with his hands gripping her soft, round hips, Tobey was behind Carmen, eagerly giving her thrust after thrust and loving every moment of it. The tattoo just above her ass was mesmerizing, drawing him in like a beacon. Her passionate moans and verbal commands had taken his confidence to all-new heights. If only for one night, the computer geek became James Bond! He did the job, and later he got the girl; the most beautiful girl he had ever seen. None of his fellow technicians would believe him, even if he gave them blow-by-blow details of his night. But that didn't matter because if he never saw Carmen again,

Tobey was smitten for life. She was everything he could ever want in a woman. Her mind was as beautiful as her body. She was intelligent, funny, and witty. And now, she was in his bed, moaning his name while riding a roller coaster of orgasmic pleasure. Neither her job nor her past mattered; just this moment.

"Fuck me, Tobey, fuck me!" Carmen commanded while thrusting her ass back against him repeatedly.
"Yes, baby, yes!" he moaned, his grip on her hips becoming stronger and his strokes becoming deeper.

For the next few hours, the two giddy lovers explored realms of plea- sure so intense that they couldn't begin to put them into words. They threw caution to the wind and as a result, they shared more orgasms than they could count.

Early the next morning, Alex found himself impatiently knocking on and jiggling the handles of the suites' double adjoining doors. When they finally opened, he was shocked to see Shavers standing there wrapped in a bed sheet with blood-shot eyes and messy hair. To Alex's surprise, he reeked of alcohol, cocoa butter, and baby oil.

What the hell happened to you?" he demanded while pushing his way past Shavers and walking into the messy suite.
"Hey Alex, how about a little courtesy, please? I mean, you can't just barge up in here like gang-busters. For all you know, I could have com- pany of something."
"You…company?" Alex scoffed before grinning uncontrollably. "Yeah, right."

Just then, Alex was suddenly stopped in his tracks by the thick, cara- mel-colored beauty lying on Shaver's bed. *What the fuck?* he thought when their eyes met. *Am I dreaming?* With his head tilted and his mouth wide open, Alex watched as she stepped out of bed and waved before disappearing into the bathroom. The man in him could not help but admire her luscious, naked frame or her round, jiggling tits. The hater in him pondered why in the hell such a woman would be interested in a geek like Shavers.

"Who the hell is she?"
Car'mel Delight," he cooed while smiling giddily at the closed door.

For the rest of this story, read the upcoming book *Operation Cover-Up: Rise of the Black Mamba* by P D Baldwin.

Brandon and Toni

A chance reunion on Face-book was just a prelude for things to come. After weeks of hearing about Toni's failed marriage, four years of celibacy, and agonizing sexual frustration, Brandon was eager to help her make up for lost time. They had only seen each other twice since reconnecting two months ago. Though twenty years had passed since that rainy October night in his parent's basement, Toni was still gorgeous. Two decades and a child hadn't spoiled her figure. In fact, it turned her tender and petite sixteen-year-old body into a curvaceous, thirty-six-year old Amazon's body! Her plump, 36Ds rode high underneath the pink V-neck sweater she was wearing a couple of weeks ago. Her black skirt hugged her voluptuous thighs and boda-cious ass. Brandon found it hard to hide the throbbing erection that was beating against the zipper of his jeans. Feeling her tits against his chest when she hugged him goodbye almost gave it away.

He wasn't the only one feeling nostalgia's effects though. The athletic eighteen-year-old boy who stole her heart and took her innocence had grown into a handsome, well-kept middle-aged man. Despite being a single dad of one and the owner/operator of his own Real Estate Company, he was in great shape. His strong arms and rock-hard chest left her gasping for air after just one hug. After a few minutes of chat-ter and laughter, Toni began to wonder why she had decided to dump him in the first place. He seemed to be more of a man than Gerald, the one she left him for and eventually settled down with.

Night after night for the next few weeks they lay awake, exchanging provocative text messages that detailed their inner most desires. It took a while to get past her shyness, but Brandon finally convinced Toni to send him some naked pictures. He couldn't help but fawn over her large round tits and the dark nipples that adorned them. He fantasized about sucking them just like he did when he was a teenager. Toni's thick thighs and round ass made him want to pound her neatly shaved pussy from the front and the back. When Brandon asked if she had any sexual hang-ups, Toni simply replied, "Let's just test the waters and see what happens. Anything is possible if the mood is right."

It had been twenty years since Brandon has taken her virginity. At long last, the night arrived for them to relive that moment. By the time he parked his G35 in front of Toni's apartment building, his dick was standing at full attention. When he got to the door and saw her standing there in a light-blue bathrobe, his heart started racing. Her smile was more beautiful than he remembered. Her long hair was up in a black clip. The way her robe hugged and outlined her frame made him want to fuck her right there on the stairs. Panic set in when he felt pre-cum gathering at the head of his dick and creating moisture in his shorts.

"*Please don't cum too quickly,*" he pleaded silently with his dick while watching her ass sway from side-to-side while walking up the stairs in front of him.

When they reached the inside of her apartment, the mood was already set. The lights were off, soft music was playing, and scented candles were burning.

"My baby fell asleep in my bed. Do you mind if we chill in here?" she asked softly while patting the couch cushion and beckoning for him to join her.

"That's cool," he replied before sitting down and taking off his shoes.

After a few moments of smiles, stares, and small talk, they were at a deadlock. All the anticipation leading up to this point threatened to leave them unfulfilled and even more frustrated. Both Brandon and Toni could feel the window of opportunity closing, but neither of them was willing to make the first move.

"I like your shorts. I think you should take them off," she said after finally taking the lead.
"Gladly," Brandon replied, for lack of a better response.

When he stood up, Toni stood up as well and untied her robe so that he could see what was hidden inside. Her soft round tits were the picture of perfection. He could barely get his shorts off before his mouth was locked onto her nipple. The intensity of his sucking nearly made her knees buckle. The sensation of his tongue circling and teasing her chocolate crowns had cum running down her inner thighs. While holding and caressing the back of his head, Toni thrust her tits into his mouth, one after the other. When his feast ended, she stepped back and dropped the robe on the floor. While catching her breath, she took in the fine, chocolate-colored brother in front of her. His big, throbbing dick was standing at full attention, beckoning for her tender touch.

"Let me get that for you," she said when she saw the glistening bubble forming at its tip.

Before Brandon could say a word, Toni had squatted in front of him. With one hand on his thigh and the other stroking his shaft, Toni began her own feast. His eyes rolled into the back of his head as her lips and tongue kissed and teased his swollen dick. Toni's grip on him as he slid in and out of her mouth had Brandon ready to unleash a torrent of lava into the back of her throat. Though he tried to fight it, he couldn't resist the urge to grab the back of her head while fucking her eager mouth.

"I want that dick inside me, Brandon," she cooed after releasing it and catching her breath again.

He watched in awe as she lay back on the floor fingering her glistening pussy. As soon as he slid the Magnum on, Brandon was deep inside Toni, thrusting slowly between her tight, wet walls. It was like déjà vu for both of them! Just like that magical night twenty years ago, they were on the floor engaging in a passionate interlude. And like then, they were trying their best to keep quiet, but they couldn't. It felt too damned good! His chocolate skin had melted together with her caramel skin once again in a hot, lust-filled dance of passion and ecstasy.

"Fuck me harder, Brandon! Pound this pussy like you said you would," Toni pled, gasping as his dick swelled deep inside her.
"Turn around, baby," he demanded before sliding his dick out and guiding her into his favorite position.

The sensation of his dick sliding in and out of her pussy while his balls banged her clit brought tears to Toni's eyes. She already had lost count of how many times she had cum while yet another orgasm was quickly taking hold of her entire body. When he smacked her ass, she almost let out a moan that would surely have awoken her sleeping son, not to mention the rest of the building. The second smack made her bite down hard on the robe that was bunched up under her head. His grip on her juicy hips was powerful and purposeful. In fact, if it hadn't been for his grip on her thighs, Brandon's feverish pounding and swollen dick would have made Toni collapse. He was determined to give her all-of-the dick he had been promising since they reconnected. Determined to make him surrender his repressed moans, Toni threw her ass back against him, pounding her dripping pussy on his dick which threatened to erupt at any minute.

"Toni," he cried repeatedly through muffled breaths.
"Give me dat nut, Brandon! Give it to me!"

That last series of thrusts, all of them deep, hard, and fast were all Toni needed to send her over the edge. Her dam broke one last time, showering his dick, balls, and thighs with her hot, milky cum. They fought hard for the next few minutes not to scream before finally settling down on the floor. They say things get better with time, and Toni and Brandon just proved it.

"I want more," he whispered while kissing her down the center of her back.
"Damn, Brandon. Gerald never touched me like that."
"From what I understand, he barely touched you at all. And that's sad because there's so much sexiness here to explore."
"Really, now?" she gasped as his fingers slowly teased her quivering clit.
"Oh, yes. Now turn over for me."
"An encore, already?" she asked when she heard his command.

When her back hit the floor, his mouth was once again locked on her tits. His tongue circled her nipples with an intensity that was more feverish than before. Toni's back arched as Brandon fingered her pussy while kissing her down her stomach. Feeling his lips going lower and lower, she guided Brandon's head to the center of her thighs where his soft kisses were replaced by flicks of his wet tongue. Before Toni could catch her breath, he had settled between her quivering thighs and placed her legs on his shoulders. The ways his tongue teased and licked her pussy were hypnotic. The ways his lips pulled and sucked on her swollen clit made Toni want to cry. With one hand caressing her tits and the other on the back of his head, she filled Brandon's mouth with wave after wave of creamy pleasure.

"Grab your ankles and hold your legs up for me, baby."
"Fuck, Brandon! *Shit!* What are you doing to me?" Toni whined while he sucked on her clit and gently fingered her puckered asshole.
"I'm testing the waters," he replied before lapping up her spilling juices.

Though thoughts of a man's dick inside her ass were taboo, Brandon was testing the waters, and Toni was enjoying every minute of it. She couldn't believe what he was doing to her or how good it felt. She had never been so free with Gerald, even though she had vowed to spend the rest of her life with him. He never showed her the passion or the attention that Brandon was showing her right now. Her guilty pleasure made her wonder just how much he was going to test the waters, but she dared not ask. Moments later, Toni found out. While she stroked her clit and held one ankle, Brandon placed her other leg back on his shoulder and began teasing her pussy and ass with the head of his throbbing dick.

"Put it in my ass!" she demanded when she felt him moving back and forth against its opening, going in a little deeper with each stroke until his head was inside.

The combined sensations of his thumb strumming her clit while making passionate love to her ass was so euphoric that Toni nearly passed out. The pressure of Brandon's dick teasing her G-spot however, kept her going and cumming at the same time. Her juices were flowing like a river now as he held both her ankles while her nails dug into his chest and shoulders. With her back arched and passionate moans escaping her mouth, Toni suddenly felt him swelling against the walls of her tender ass. Her head almost exploded when she felt the rush of his hot lava flowing inside her. Just when she threatened to cry out, Brandon kissed her lips, inhaling her passionate screams while tears of ecstasy flowed from her eyes. Her body quivered and her heart pounded as his dick danced and spewed warm cream inside her ass.

"I love you, Brandon," she surrendered when he slumped beside her and pulled her body close to his.
"Mommy, are you in there?" called the squeaky voice from the hallway as Brandon kissed her shoulder while squeezing her soft tits.

That Night...

There are nights in your life you pray would never end.
For me it was the night I made love to my best friend.

We stole a few moments to escape the world,
Walking along hand in hand, you and me; a boy and a girl.

Her eyes shimmered like diamonds. Her skin was as soft as silk.
The taste of her lips was like honey; her body against mine like warm milk.

Looking into her eyes made my heart race out of control.
I love this woman from the depths of my heart clear down to my soul.

The atmosphere was thick, romance was in the air.
Her call to me was subliminal, taunting me like a dare.

Her skirt was long and flowing around hips so soft and creamy.
Just thinking about that ass underneath had my body all hot and steamy.

With a look of love in her eyes and a sexy smile on her face,
It didn't matter that we were outside. I had to have her in this place.

Once again her body taunted me, her eyes so full of desire.
With a swing of her hips and a grind on my lap, she lit one hell of a fire.

Taunting me and teasing me with a lap dance straight from hell,
She dared me with her eyes to insert what she knew had swelled.

Accepting her dare and ignoring our surroundings,
I slid myself inside to begin my passionate pounding.

She slowed whined it on me, grinded on me, made me cry out her name.
A man became a boy, but my cries had no shame.

The passion in the air covered our bodies in a warm exotic mist.
We moved our bodies to a rhythm as our lips passionately kissed.

Our eyes met briefly as she slowly arched her spine.
Explosions within us erupted as I held her body close to mine.

I told myself if I had the chance, my life with her I'd spend.
But nothing could be as beautiful as the night I made love to my best friend.

Leo and Yvette

As he walked down the hall reading a message on his Blackberry, the last person Leo expected to see coming out of his bank's new-hire class was Yvette, the one that got away. From the time they were kids, he secretly loved her but she was more interested in beating him up than being his girlfriend. Then when they went to high school, she was the popular "in-crowd" girl, while Leo became one of the resident nerds. Besides, Yvette was madly in love with Andre, the high school "All-American" whom she eventually married and who later fathered her children. They shared a glimmer of hope about eight years ago, however. Yvette and Andre had separated forcing her to move back in with her parents, who just so happened to live up the street from Leo. After seeing her hanging around for a few days, curiosity got the best of him and he finally went up to the door.

When Yvette opened it, Leo found himself at a loss for words. She was just as beautiful as the day he watched from afar while the limo whisked her away to her wedding. When she told him she was single again, the timing was perfect because he was too. Late one night while sitting on her parents' porch, Yvette decided to invite Leo up for a talk. Since it was taking place at her parents' house and not his, Leo didn't make much of it.

"You know, Leo," Yvette began while sitting next to him in the cool night air, "there's something that I've wanted to do to you for a very long time."

"Is that so?" he asked, his curiosity rising as fast as his dick. "What's that?"

"I don't know how to explain it and I'm not sure how you'll take it."

"Just go with the flow," he replied smoothly, thinking about the darkened porch and the endless possibilities.

He also remembered that his house was only a few doors down from where they were.

"Are you sure?" she asked nervously.

"I'm sure."

Seconds later, the sting from her hand crashing against his jaw had Leo's right ear ringing like the Liberty Bell. Yvette had just slapped the shit out of him and she was smiling about it.

"It's your fault. It should have been you, not Andre!"

Under normal circumstances, an ass whuppin' would have been the next course of action, but Leo remembered all the torture he had inflicted on his childhood sweetheart. He also remembered conceding her heart to his adversary, instead of telling her how he felt. Seeing that Yvette was about to leap off the porch, Leo took a deep breath and smiled at her.

"You know, Yvette," he began when he took her gently by the hand and pulled her close, "there's something I've been wanting to do to you since we were kids too."

"Oh hell, no!" she said before bursting into a fit of laughter while trying to flee inside.

"I'm serious, Yvette, and no I'm not going to slap the shit out of you like you just did to me. Please come and sit back down."

"Leo, I swear if you hit me, I'm gonna kill you," she replied before slowly sitting back down with her fists balled-up.

"You have my word," he said, with a look his in eyes that was so intense she couldn't help but wonder what was next.

"What is it?"

"This," he replied before taking Yvette in his arms and passionately kissing her lips.

This kiss, their first kiss, seemed to last for an eternity. His tongue explored her mouth while his hand found its way to her thigh, and up to her tit where it squeezed and caressed before coming to a rest on her cheek.

"Damn, Leo. It's been a long time since a kiss made my pussy wet."

"I want you. Yvette, I always have. I wanna be your man. I don't wanna just have sex and let it end there. I wanna do it right this time. I want the chance to date and romance you. Can I take you out tomorrow night, or is that too soon?"

"Leo, I didn't know you felt so strongly about this. I'd love to go out with you. I'll have my parents watch Brit for me."

"I'll pick you up at eight, but before I go, can I have another kiss?" he asked while leaning in again.

"Just be patient 'til tomorrow and I'll give you more than that, baby," she whispered after placing her index finger over his lips and smiling.

Tomorrow never came. Before Leo could arrive, Andre came to reclaim his wife. Leo and Yvette hadn't spoken since. Now eight years later, here she was, walking down the hall towards him. Once again Leo found himself at a loss for words. She was still as beautiful as she was that night on the porch. Overcome with anxiety, he tried to duck into an empty conference room, but it was too late. She had already seen him.

"Leo?" called that all too familiar voice. "OMG, I can't believe it's you!

"Yeah... um... what's up, Yvette?" he asked reluctantly.

"I'll catch up with y'all later. I wanna catch up with my old friend," she said to a group of curious ladies.

"So, I guess you're about to start working here, huh?"

"Yep. Being a stay-at-home mom / real-estate appraiser just isn't paying the bills anymore. Besides, with the kids in school, I needed something to do."

"Kids?" Leo asked almost in shock. "I thought you only had Brit."

"Time flies babe. I've had two more since then."

You'd never know it, he thought, unable to keep his eyes from admiring her curvaceous frame. "I'll bet Andre enjoyed making them."

"Andre hasn't enjoyed much else in over a year, though. We're separated again."

"That's too bad," Leo replied, pretending not to care.

Though he didn't like Andre and found himself wanting another chance with Yvette, he wasn't about to set himself up for failure again.

"I fucked up that night on the porch. I should never have taken him back, but I wanted my baby to be with her father, and I did everything I could to make it work. But nothing worked, especially since I was the only one trying."

"Why are you telling me this, Yvette?"

"Because I'm standing here realizing that after all this time, I still love you."

"I love you too," he surrendered, unable to stop the words from escaping his mouth.

Soon afterwards, a courtship began, and after three months of texting, flirting, and sexually explicit late-night phone talk, they found themselves alone on the waterfront. The 2:00 a.m. air was nice and cool; a perfect contrast to the heat their bodies were generating. Yvette's long white skirt blew freely in the breeze, accentuating her wide, curvaceous hips and round ass. Meanwhile, Leo was lost in the moment, admiring her beauty and the glimmer in her hazel eyes. He sat quietly on the wall behind her, watching as she danced to the slow, sexy beat that was playing in her head. Moments later, she was inches from him, still dancing and gyrating while caressing and massaging her breasts through her wife beater.

Yvette's ass and thighs felt so warm and soft when she sat on his lap and began grinding back and forth, nice and slow. Her hot, wet pussy hovered right over the head of his throbbing dick, which was beating furiously against his zipper. He knew by the position she was in that she felt him craving to be inside her. Her grinding became more of a taunt when she bent over and grabbed her ankles. She raised her ass up just enough for Leo to pull her skirt up around her waist which revealed her voluptuous, naked ass. It was a sight to behold! Yvette's soft skin glowed in the moonlight. He could see the juices from her pussy leaving a milky pool on the front of his black jeans. Though she never said a word, Yvette was daring him to enter her. After a brief struggle with his belt buckle and zipper, Leo pulled his dick out. Rising again, Yvette waited anxiously until his head parted her pulsating lips. When she felt it, she dropped it like it was hot, taking every inch of Leo's dick into her pussy at once.

Damn! she thought.

She couldn't believe how hard it was. Nothing she could have imagined prepared her for what she felt so deep inside her right now. Leo's dick was perfect: long, thick, and throbbing. She could feel every vein, crease, and inch as she slid up and down his pole. The slap of his balls against her clit was quickly becoming intoxicating. As if it had built in radar, his dick head quickly found her G-spot. No matter how she moved, Leo's dick was right there, sending chills up and down her spine while she drenched his balls with cum. The sensation of his tight grip on her thighs as he thrust upwards had her pussy on fire. Neither of them cared that just across the street beyond some trees, railroad tracks, and a busy street was a luxury condominium development. At any moment, a random passerby could have happened upon them, but they didn't care. What they felt was too intense to think about stopping now.

Leo's hands snaked underneath Yvette's wife beater and found their way to her breasts, which he caressed and squeezed while guiding her up and down on his swollen dick. The vibrations of her walls and the flow of her river down his shaft made Leo explode deep inside her. Yvette wondered if she would be able to hold all the lava that seemed to keep gushing from his dick. Passionate sighs and soft moans escaped her lips as she leaned back and felt him gently kissing her goose-bump-covered shoulder.

"Damn, Leo," she exhaled before standing up and pulling her skirt down.

"Wow," was all he could manage while staring at his glistening, dripping dick.

"So, baby, was I worth the wait?" Yvette asked when she sat next to him.

The sight of her there with her feet on the wall with her long legs and juicy thighs spread-eagle had Leo hypnotized. Her pussy and ass were so beautiful that his fingers couldn't help but explore everything she hid underneath her skirt.

"It's all in place," she smiled when his middle finger grazed her puckered asshole. "Is that all you have for me?"

"Nope," Leo replied before taking her by the hand and leading her to the shelter on the other side of the walkway.

Their hearts and minds began racing the second they stepped inside. The walls inside the shelter were made of mirrors that stretched from its floor to its ceiling. Behind them, in front of them, and above them was nothing but their own reflections. As Leo stood behind her with his dick pressed against her ass, their senses went into orgasmic overload. Instinctively, Yvette bent over and gripped the bench in front her, anticipating him being deep inside her once again, and within seconds, his dick was thrusting in and out of her pussy. The look of intensity on his face when she saw his reflection was intoxicating. She couldn't help but scream his name while he repeatedly smacked her bouncing, light-caramel-colored ass.

"Fuck me, Leo, fuck me harder!" Yvette demanded.

Even in the darkness of night, there was enough light reflecting off the mirrors to give him a perfect view of her ass and the sexy faces she was making, which made him pound her pussy faster and harder. Those looks said it all. She was loving every stroke of his dick. He slowed his strokes periodically so he could watch his dick disappear inside Yvette's pussy.

Feeling it swell and his load slowly course up through his shaft, Leo pounded Yvette's pussy relentlessly making the shelter echo with the sounds of colliding flesh and passionate moans. With one last thrust, Leo once again filled her pussy with blast after blast of hot bubbling lava, which when it collided with hers, spilled out and splashed on the ground at her feet. If he hadn't been holding her hips so tightly, Yvette would surely have collapsed to the ground from her weakened knees. After milking him dry, and catching her breath, she stood up and looked into her lover's eyes. This kiss was more electrifying than their first. After years of allowing the curiosity and anticipation to build, they allowed their passion to run wild. This night would prove to be the first of many such encounters.

The Bet

"These hands?" Sean asked in shock and awe while staring into his quivering palms.

"Yes, Sean, those hands," Kayla replied. "A bet is a bet, remember? Anything your hands can touch your eyes can see."

Ah yes, the bet. The bet itself was simple. If her team won the NBA finals, Sean had to treat her to dinner and a movie. After that, he had to give her a full body massage. If his team won, Kayla had to strip for him and give him a private showing of the body he had openly lusted after for years. In the aftermath of his team winning the NBA title in six games, Kayla was at his house to settle her debt, one he would have let her out of simply out of respect for their friendship. Little did they know that what turned out to be a simple wager was about to change their lives forever. His hesitation, however, threatened to let his once-in-a-lifetime moment to see her in her full naked glory slip away.

"Maybe now isn't the right time," she said nervously after studying his apprehension.

"There's no time like the present," Sean replied when he stood up and walked towards her.

After looking deeply into her beautiful brown eyes, he kissed her soft lips with a passion that took her senses by storm. She knew that they shared a strong, physical attraction, but this kiss was different. It was the kind of kiss a man gives his lover. He gently caressed her shoulders as their tongues danced slowly and passionately, inhaling her soft moans while tasting her soft wet tongue. His hands moved slowly down her arms and back up, squeezing and caressing her large, round H-cup tits. Her bulging nipples hardened in his palms, causing his dick to tingle in his shorts. After a few moments, his hands made their way from Kayla's breasts down to her thighs, where again they squeezed and caressed before moving around and doing the same to her soft, voluptuous ass. With his message clearly sent, Sean stepped back and looked at the chocolate beauty before him.

"Are you sure you can handle all that?" she asked while turning slowly and seductively from side-to-side.
"I'm willing to find out," he replied before stepping back a little farther to take in all of her sexiness.

Her hands traced the same path as his, gently squeezing and caressing her tits before moving down her stomach and unbuttoning her faded blue jeans. The zipper couldn't open fast enough. The sight of her white cotton panties as she pushed her jeans down her chocolate colored hips had his heart racing. When she stepped out and kicked them to the side, Kayla could see that his dick had swollen beneath his white T-shirt. Sean watched with eager anticipation while she undid the top two buttons on her pink sweater before lifting it over her head and dropping it to the floor. The white bra she was wearing barely seemed capable of containing her massive tits.

"Wanna help me unhook my bra?" Kayla asked softly after turning around and peering over her shoulder at him.

With his dick throbbing and pre-cum bubbling at its tip, Sean walked up behind her. With his dick was pressed firmly against the crack of her ass, He reached under Kayla's arms so that he could squeeze and caress her tits again. He couldn't believe this was happening. She was almost naked in his house and he was savoring every single moment. After a few more minutes of caressing and planting soft kisses on her trembling shoulders, Sean unhooked her bra. With her straps out of the way, he kissed Kayla down her spine while slowly sliding her panties off her ass and down her hips. What was before his eyes was nothing short of exquisite. Her round, chocolate ass was sexier than he could have ever imagined. His kisses on it and her thighs sent shudders throughout Kayla's entire body, and made it scream for more. After standing up and stepping back, Sean watched her turn around slowly with her arms folded across her melons, keeping her from revealing her total bounty. After a few moments of teasing she unfolded her arms, releasing her bra and letting it fall to the floor.

Sean was frozen. Nothing could have prepared him for what he as seeing. Kayla was sexier and shapelier than he could have ever imagined. Her body was perfect. Her breasts were capped by large round nipples in a darker shade of chocolate than her skin. Her pussy hairs were short enough to reveal the sexy, pouting flesh beneath them. His amazement, however, made Kayla nervous. Sean's constant bouts of apprehension made her think the opposite. She was very self-conscious about her weight, size, and shape, and his lack of words didn't help her confidence either. She assumed that he didn't like what he was seeing and nervously broke eye contact to begin looking for her clothes.

"Maybe I should get dressed."
"Not at all," Sean replied before walking up to Kayla again, taking her in his arms, and kissing her more passionately than he had earlier.

Before Kayla could catch her breath, she was lying on the floor with Sean on top of her, feverishly licking and sucking her hardened nipples. Her wet pussy was saturating the front of his shorts, causing his dick to jump as her juices spread across the material.

"I'd feel better about being naked if you were too."
"Oh yeah," Sean replied, having forgotten that he was still dressed.

When he stood up, he got a full, enticing view of her luscious body. Her clit glistened when she ran her fingers across it, teasing it while moaning softly. His dick throbbed with anticipation while watching her other hand gently glide across her tits. When he dropped to his knees, Sean began planting soft wet kisses on Kayla's feet, then moving slowly up her legs and onto her thighs. Though his dick wanted to be deep inside her, his tongue had other plans. The farther he moved up her thigh, the more her body ached for him. Without warning, he parted her thighs and began feasting on her glistening peach. He sucked and licked Kayla's clit with the same passion and intensity as he had her nipples. She could barely breathe when she felt his tongue circling and teasing her thick, juicy lips. Lifting her legs onto his shoulders, Sean tongue fucked her pussy while teasing her asshole with his thumb. She cried out in orgasmic euphoria as he lapped her juices up like a lion at a watering hole. Kayla was cumming so hard and fast that she found herself praying that Sean wouldn't drown.

"I've wanted you for longer than I can remember," he gasped when he finally slid his dick into her hot pussy, teasing her with the head before feeding her slow, deep strokes.
"I want you too, baby! It is good to you baby?" she whined as his throbbing dick massaged her tight, wet sugar walls.
"Yes," he gasped.
"Is it tight enough for you?" she cooed.
"Yes!"
"Is it wet enough for you, baby?"
"Oh, hell yes!" he surrendered with pressure building in his hard, thrusting shaft.

With his body pressed tight to hers, Sean was living out his ultimate sexual fantasy. He was making love to the woman whom he had secretly lusted for since high school. Though he had gotten close to her in college, it was nothing like this. They never went any further than some kissing and fondling, but now it was full-blown, erotic love making. Her moans were like music to his ears. The rake of her nails across his back fueled his intensity as he pounded her sweet black pussy. Sean fought hard against nature while looking into Kayla's eyes and kissing her lips. He slowed his strokes when his dick threatened to betray him prematurely. He lifted her legs onto his shoulders and kissed her calves while sucking her toes and continuing to feed her pussy stroke after stroke. He wanted and needed to leave an impression on this thick, sexy vixen. He had to have her again and again. Her body felt incredible next to his, her pussy engulfing every inch of his thrusting dick.

With each stroke, Kayla felt her milky rain flowing freely from her pussy, down the crack of her ass, and pooling beneath her. The constant thrust of his dick and her back moving against the floor added to her erotic sensation. She knew she was going to have rug burns later, but her body was so on fire with passion and desire for Sean, she didn't care. Each rapid-fire climax caused his name to escape her trembling lips. All her fears and anxieties about her body were quickly laid to rest. It was clear by his strokes, his moans, and the way he touched her body that Sean loved everything she had to offer. His touch was so passionate that Kayla could feel her moans getting louder and louder. She was sure that with the windows open, someone was bound to hear her calling his name. She didn't care though. She was enjoying Sean as much as he was enjoying her. The swell of his dick between her walls sent Kayla into sensual overload. Harder and faster he pounded, moaning while gripping her ankles with his trembling hands. With one final deep thrust, Kayla felt the creamy eruption and erratic spasms of his dick inside her. Drained of cum and riding a wave of pleasure, Sean released her ankles and lay down atop Kayla, nestling his sweat-covered brow against her soft bosoms.

"Damn," they sighed silently while contemplating when, where, and how to top what they had just done.

Intoxicated

I can take it, sure I can. That's the lie I told myself.
I should have never started fucking with that shit off the top shelf.

Ever since that first hit, my life has been nothing short of pure bliss.
I should have never started fucking with that top shelf shit.

The taste is off the chain like a wine so sweet and exotic.
When it touches my tongue, it covers my body in a feeling so damned erotic.

The pull is so alluring. Like a junkie, I'm hooked on this sexy new crack.
Since I had that first hit, I'm too far gone and can't imagine not going back.

Every thought of tasting it sets my soul on fire.
The way I crave your taste is sin and yet such a sensual desire.

I'm like a virgin all over again, feeling geeked bout my first piece of ass.
Since I had a taste of you, I want nothing else in my glass.

Part of me says to put you down 'cause this feeling I just can't shake.
But the thought of not having you is a feeling I just can't take.

P D Baldwin

I should have known I wasn't ready. I guess I should have waited.
Now I'm sitting here all fucked up 'cause my heart is intoxicated.

You're coursing through my blood, being pumped by my very own heart.
I'm so hooked on this top shelf shit that it's torn my world apart.

I wanna taste you so bad right now that my body is starting to trip.
Though my body's fiending for it all, I'd settle for just a sip.

When another calls your name my heart sends out a plea.
I shouldn't have to share you because God made you for me.

I've tried to pray off my addiction or at least for the means to control to it.
This desire for you has me in such a trance because my will you up and stole it.

I know my drinking days must end 'cause I gotta get my life on track.
But the way your shit keeps calling me, I can't help but to keep looking back.

On that bottle there should be a seal, as many before me have stated.
But never would I let you go or this feeling of being intoxicated.

The Toy

"Come straight home after work," Paul said while sitting on the bed eyeing the bright red bag with the words "Hustler Hollywood" emblazoned on it in gold letters.

"A surprise for me?" she asked with giddy anticipation. "What is it?"

"It wouldn't be a surprise if I told you. Now go back to work and I'll see you later."

"You're no fun Paul," she sighed. "I'm pouting now bottom lip out and all."

"I love you too, Nikki," he mused before hanging up the phone.

Paul must have loved her very much because against his better judgment, he was about to try to make her ultimate sexual fantasy come true. Since getting together, Nikki's sexual pleasure had been Paul's personal mission, but his sexual appetite was no match for hers. At first she kept it hidden, but once Paul opened her Pandora's Box, Nikki became a sexual hurricane. Anytime place, any place; it didn't matter. If his Yukon could talk, it would have some erotic stories to tell. Over the years, they had talked about experimenting with various objects while exploring their inner most desires and wildest fantasies. One night while she was giving him head, he accidentally discovered Nikki's hidden passion for anal sex. As she knelt beside Paul with him fingering her wet pussy, his finger accidentally grazed her "forbidden zone." Though she never said a word, she let out a moan that gave it away. Suddenly, she began sucking his dick with unrivaled intensity. When he began fingering her puckered asshole, the moans Nikki let out, the vibrations from her throat, and her strokes on his shaft made Paul cum so hard and fast that he nearly passed out. Over the next few weeks, they experimented with various lubes and numerous techniques until at last he introduced her to full-blown anal sex, and Nikki loved it! Her desire for it was so intense that she began demanding it regularly. The pressure Paul's dick created against her G-spot gave her orgasms the likes of which she couldn't begin to describe. Her pussy would be wet all night after feeling Paul bust a nut in her ass.

One night as they lay in the bed together, Nikki revealed another hidden sexual desire. It involved having sex with two men at the same time. In her words, "Being dominated by two dicks at the same time would give me the ultimate orgasm." Like any normal man, the thought of another man sexing his lover made Paul's skin crawl. It didn't help that she told him that she fantasized about him being one of the men. Crossing swords with another dude was out of the question, even though it was what Nikki wanted so badly. She never forced the issue, but it lingered in the back of Paul's mind. Nikki had never denied him any of his sexual pleasures thus far, but compared to hers, his desires were rather simple.

This was totally different, though. This meant having another dick inside his woman. In an attempt satisfy his lover's desire and his own curiosity, Paul took a trip to the local 'toy store' and looked at their selection of vibrators and dildos. Though the curious stares he drew from onlookers made him hesitant to make a selection, he was determined to see cum dripping from Nikki's pussy and a smile on her face. It was worth a few minutes of embarrassment. Paul meticulously searched until he found what he was looking for: a six-inch chocolate-colored penis. After all, he didn't want to get anything larger than him for fear that she would enjoy it more than his own dick. Besides, it was just a prop. He was the real thing.

For the next few hours, Nikki agonized at work while trying to figure out what her surprise must be. It wasn't her birthday, Sweetest

Day, or their anniversary. Valentine's Day had passed, and Christmas was months away. She was stumped. At 6:30 p.m., she barely spoke to her friends while racing out of the door and to her car. Curiosity and anxiety nearly turned into road rage as she inched along in the late-evening traffic. The anticipation of what was ahead had caused moisture to soak through her panties. When she arrived at home, Paul had made dinner and was drawing her bubble bath. After rushing through dinner and bathing, she joined him in the bedroom, where his naked body lay half covered by a white satin sheet.

Dayum, she thought before taking her robe off and joining him in bed.
"Okay, baby, you've tortured me long enough. What's my surprise?"
"You'll see, sexy," he replied before kissing her on her shoulder and then her lips.
"You've been saying that shit all night. I have ways of making you talk," she said before shoving him down on the bed and snatching back the covers.

Her head was his weakness. She wasn't sure if it was the swirl of her tongue, or the way her hand slid up and down his shaft while beating his throbbing dick head against her tongue. Whatever it was, Nikki knew it was torture to him, which meant she could get anything she wanted once she started working that dick like a porno star. Shortly after she began, she knew she had him. Paul's moans were always a dead giveaway. She felt his entire body writhing in sexual agony. A few minutes more and he would be right where she wanted him; spilling his load and begging for mercy. Little did she know that Paul had made plans of his own. While her head bobbed slowly up and down on his dick, he was struggling feverishly to reach under the pillow next to her upward-pointed ass. With his dick swelling in her mouth, Nikki suddenly felt a familiar sensation that set her soul on fire. She could feel a hardened dick slowly sliding into her pussy while Paul's dick was in her mouth. She tried to gather her thoughts, but she couldn't. There was another man's dick inside her! *Who was he? Where did he come from? How did he get in?* Paul had said repeatedly that he couldn't imagine another man pleasuring her. *Had he changed his mind?*

Both Paul and Nikki struggled with their guilty pleasures. In his wildest dreams, Paul never imagined he would enjoy fucking Nikki with a dildo while she gave him head, but it was worth it if she reached the next level of intensity! *"How could the best head on the planet get even better?"* he pondered while at the same time wondering which was wetter now, her pussy or her mouth?

Though she was firmly in control of Paul's dick, Nikki's mind and body were on the verge of a total meltdown. *"Two dicks! Two dicks!"* echoed over and over in her mind as his head banged against the back of her throat. With her mouth locked on and her hand pumping his shaft like a piston, Nikki milked his dick of every drop of cum she could get. The warm feel and sweet taste of his cream splashing in the back of her throat triggered her to have her own mind-blowing orgasm. Though Paul was panting and his body shuddering uncontrollably, Nikki was determined not to let it end there. She had made up her mind that she was going to suck his dick until it was hard again. While circling and teasing his head with her tongue, Paul and his toy were still hard at work.

When she finally managed to look into the mirror at the foot of the bed, Nikki had yet another creamy orgasm that rained down her thighs and pooled at her quivering knees. The sight of Paul pleasing and teasing her with a dildo sent orgasmic currents racing through her entire body, while giving her a natural high at the same time.

"I want your dick inside me now, Paul!" she gasped while looking into his eyes and stroking his rigid shaft.
"Hell yeah, baby!"

Within moments, Paul was behind her, pounding her pussy with his hard, throbbing dick. The sensations from earlier were still firing throughout Nikki's body as she clutched the sheets and called out his name. Goose bumps and perspiration erupted all over her flesh while each stroke brought her closer to her next climax. The way Paul was switching up the speed and depth of his strokes had Nikki dizzy. The sensation of him swelling again while squeezing and caressing her soft hips was bringing tears to her eyes. Suddenly, she felt baby oil being rubbed on and squirted into her ass. It wouldn't be long now before Paul was treating her ass to the same treat as her pussy. Chills raced up and down her spine when his thumb circled and teased her asshole before finally sliding inside. Nikki loved every moment of it! When another orgasm began to swell inside her walls, Paul slid his thumb out and began teasing her with the dildo.

"Oh my gawd!" Nikki cried when she felt its head slowly entering her pulsating, oil-coated ass.

Upon its entry, the initial feeling of pressure and discomfort lasted only for a few seconds before it was quickly replaced by intense pleasure. Two dicks were at work inside her; one in her pussy and one in her ass! It was hypnotic. With her face buried in a pillow, Nikki begged Paul not to stop. While on the verge of passing out and gasping for air, she wondered who was enjoying this more; her or him? After pulling the dildo out and tossing it aside, Paul slid his dick into Nikki's ass and began his own pounding. She loved his thrusts. The power, speed, and intensity made her call out his name! She played with her clit while he smacked and fucked her ass passionately.

With a final cry of "Nikki!" he released a torrent of hot, bubbling, cum inside her asshole. Spent and out of breath, Nikki collapsed on the bed with Paul on her back. With his dick still buried inside her, Paul held her hands while kissing her back and shoulders. Smiling and squeezing his hands, Nikki kissed his cheek before drifting off to sleep. Her lover had fulfilled her fantasy by giving her the ultimate satisfaction.

Let Me Seduce You

I've been waiting to seduce you since the first time we met,
Making passionate love to your body like it's the last chance I'll get.

I wanna touch and kiss your body make it all warm and wet.
With you I wanna share passion that neither of us will forget.

Girl, when this night is over, on this you can surely bet.
When I'm done loving you down, you won't have a single regret.

And when the morning comes and we look back on last night's pleasure,
The piece of you I take is one I'll always treasure.

Let me seduce you.

Your bubble bath is ready, full of water so hot and steamy.
When you're done, I'll rub your body with oil and lotion so creamy.

With your body submerged in water, your skin begins to glow.
Sip on this champagne, baby, while I bathe you nice and slow.

The sponge is soft and moist as it glides across your skin.
"What are your plans for me?" you ask which I answer with a grin.

"I asked you a question, baby, with my feelings you shouldn't toy."

"That's for me to know, my lover, and for you to simply enjoy."

Let me seduce you.

Now we're standing in the bedroom me patting you dry with a towel.
I stand behind you caressing, while in your ear I seductively growl.

"I want you." "Not yet," I interrupt, my finger pressed softly to your lips.
Taking a step back, your body's against mine with your ass massaging my hips.

I lay you down softly, slowly, and gently on a bed all covered in roses.
In my mind I can see your body in all sorts of sexy poses.

Like a snake I slither down your skin leaving a trail with my tongue and lips.
I kiss down your stomach and across your thighs before settling between your hips.

Let me seduce you.

Your hips rise and fall as you caress my ears and rub the back of my head.
You bite your lip and call out my name as your juices spill onto the bed.

"Take me, I'm yours. Don't make me wait. Baby, don't tease me this way."
"You have me so hot I'm starting to shake," are the words I hear you say.

I make my way back up, my body on yours as our tongues become intertwined.
You open your legs and wrap them around me as we slowly start to grind.

Before I slide in, I pause and relax 'cause there's so much of you to explore.
I kiss on your neck and suck on your breasts as I throb near your open door.

Let me seduce you.

The deeper I thrust, the more you love it. Now our bodies are covered in sweat.
You feel so damned good wrapped tightly around me with your insides so warm and wet.

"Fuck me hard and make me cum!" you demand as I place your legs on my shoulders.
Each passionate stroke makes you more vocal as your demands become even bolder.

Now lie on your stomach and just relax as my tongue goes up and down your spine.
Now raise your hips and back it up a little so I can take you from behind.

With my hands on your waist, I thrust deep inside as I gently smack your ass.
"Tell me, baby, how do want it? Would you like me to do it slow or fast?"

Let me seduce you.

Now I'm on my back, and you're on top. You're working it hard and fast.
I grab your hips to slow you down. I don't know if I'm going to last.

"Work it however you want it," I say as your nails dig into my chest.
My head is spinning, and I'm gasping for air as I reach up and squeeze your breasts.

Like two volcanoes, our bodies erupt when you sit up and arch your back.

You rub on your breasts as you exhale, and our bodies begin to relax.

Now that we're done, lie next to me so I can hold you near.
With my hand on your waist, I'll kiss your shoulder and whisper, "I love you, my dear."

Let me seduce you.

Naughty Co-Workers

The first time David laid eyes on Brianna, he knew he had to have her. Though the short, full-figured goddess was new to the call center where he worked, and it was full of beautiful woman, she quickly became the center of attention. Her body was a sight to behold: round, 36" DD tits, a voluptuous ass, juicy thighs, and a face beautiful enough to shame any model. The soft tone of her voice was as poetic as it was erotic. Whether her long, auburn hair was in a ponytail or down on her shoulders, it didn't matter. Brianna was gorgeous. Having earned the reputation of the department playboy, David hoped that the haters wouldn't taint her opinions of him. Most of the stories they were telling about him were lies anyway.

Not wanting to come on too strong, yet still show his interest, David carefully observed Brianna over a period of weeks. He quickly discovered who she hung out with, her hobbies, when she took breaks, and even her favorite snacks. He also learned where she liked to park in the garage and the year, make, and model of her car; a silver 2006 Mazda 6s.

After weeks of flirtation and surveillance, it was time to make his move. On a cold November day after running over some road debris on the way from lunch, Brianna's front passenger-side tire was as flat as a slice of bread. Having missed his opportunity to escort her outside due to an extended call, David walked out alone and pissed off. As he walked up the stairs in the frigid garage, he heard Brianna's frantic voice.

When he walked up to her, she was on the phone with a representative from her insurance company.

"What do you mean, it'll take an hour? It's freezing out here!"
"Are you okay, Brianna?"
"My tire is flat and help won't be here for at least an hour."
"A flat tire, huh? Is that all? Hang that up. I got this, boo."
"I'll call you back," she said after David disappeared up the stairs.

Moments later, Brianna heard the Isley Brothers echoing throughout the garage and within seconds, David's white Nissan Armada pulled up next to her car.

"Get in and warm up while I change your tire," he said after lowering the tinted passenger glass. "You got a spare, right?"
"Yeah, but I don't have a jack."
"Relax, boo. I told you I got this," he said while smiling and motioning for her to get in.
"Okay," she replied with a smile.

Her heart was all a flutter at the thought of her knight in shining armor coming to her rescue. From the cozy warmth of his truck, Brianna watched David jack her car up and go to work. By now the temperature had dropped well below freezing and part of her was saddened when she saw steam billowing from his mouth and nose. David didn't seem bothered by it though. In fact, he was on a mission. He quickly removed the flat and replaced it with the donut spare. She wasn't sure if it was him taking charge of her situation, the music, or the heat from the leather seat below her ass. It may have been a combination of the three, but whatever it was, it was making her pussy wet and her nipples hard. After David had finished and put his tools away, he returned to the front seat to find Brianna sitting there relaxed and smiling. She had taken off her coat which gave him a perfect view of her sumptuous bust line, especially since she was wearing such a low-cut red sweater. Red was his favorite color.

"All done," he said, trying his best not to stare after removing his gloves and placing his hands in over the dashboard vent.
"You're my hero," she cooed before cupping his hands in hers and blowing warm breath on them.

When her mouth opened and the warm air entered his hands, David's dick rose to full attention. Images of Brianna's lips wrapped around it swirled through in his mind while she massaged his hands and looked into his lust-filled eyes.

"It was my pleasure," he replied while secretly wishing his dick was the next in line to feel the warmth of her mouth. "I'd be happy to follow you home, ya know to make sure nothing else goes wrong, that is."
"Forever the gentleman," Brianna replied before placing soft, warm kisses on his icy fingertips.

Minutes later, after her car warmed up, Brianna left the garage with David in tow. A short while later, they drove into her parking lot where he watched her get out and run into the building. After she stood in the doorway and blew him a kiss, reality set in. For all his hard work, David had no apartment number and no phone number! He wanted to kick himself while driving home. The next day however, his chivalry paid off.

While David sat alone at the table eating lunch, the events of the previous night played over and over in his head. He thought of at least a thousand things he could have done differently, each ending with him spending the night fucking the shit out of Brianna. Just as he was about to stand up, he saw her coming across the cafeteria towards him. It was casual Friday, and she was wearing a red turtle neck under a blue blazer and faded, form-fitting jeans. Her entire body, especially her tits looked more delicious than the night before.

He sat back down hoping she hadn't seen the rapid rise taking place inside his jeans.

"Leaving so soon?" she asked with a bit of disappointment in her voice.
"I suddenly found a few reasons to stay," he replied after glancing at her tits.
"I really want to thank you for last night. Not many guys would have stood out in the cold changing a flat for girl like you did. That was really sweet."
"It was my pleasure, Brianna. Really, it was no trouble."
"I know it's short notice, but do you have plans for tonight? I was hoping you could come over and watch some movies with me."

Her words set off fireworks. At long last, she was inviting him to her house. Now, it was just a matter of time.

"I don't have any plans, and I'd love to."
"Cool," she replied, sounding very relieved. "You already know the address. Here is my apartment number and phone number. Call me if anything changes. Is ten good for you?"
"Trust me, nothing is going to change, and ten is just fine," he replied before picking the paper up off the table and memorizing it.

That night after leaving work, the time couldn't pass fast enough. While pacing back and forth in his apartment, David thought repeatedly about how he was going to seduce Brianna. His plan was to arrive by ten, make some small talk, lay his game down, and by eleven they would be listening to a mix of music from his smart phone while he waxed her bodacious, butter-scotch ass. At 9:45 p.m., he shot her a text, and by 10:00 p.m., he was at her building. To his delight, Brianna was standing by the door in a long pink bathrobe. The thought of her naked underneath it made his dick throb with anticipation. He had fantasized about the luscious delights that lay underneath those layers of clothing. Even in the cold, her smile was electric. He stared at her ass as it swayed back and forth on the way down the hall. When he got inside her apartment, the lights were low and candles were burning.

"Have a seat and let me take your coat."

David sat on the couch and watched while Brianna hung his coat up before sitting in the chair next to him. When she removed her pink robe, David forgot all the plans that he had laid out. Her peaks and valleys were gorgeous! Her white "Hello Kitty" shirt and black boy shorts clung so tightly to her curvaceous frame that they looked like her skin. As they sat there with a movie playing, David couldn't figure out which part of her body he wanted to savor the most: her sexy lips, her large luscious tits, her juicy ass, or all of the above. Pre-cum had already begun to pool at the tip of his dick, which he tried to conceal by crossing his legs. He was afraid that it would explode as soon as he slid it inside her. Thirty minutes passed before David realized that he had no idea what they were supposed to be watching, nor did he care. He couldn't stop staring at Brianna, no matter how hard he tried. Meanwhile, after recognizing that she had his full attention Brianna stopped the movie and turned the television off.

"Would you like some head?"
"Huh?"
"I asked if you want me to suck your dick? I see the way you've been looking at me," she said, smiling as she stood up and walked over to him.

Before David could respond, Brianna was kneeling between his legs and undoing the string on his dark gray jogging pants. She looked into his eyes and smiled when she pulled his dick out and stroked it, admiring it when it swelled in her hand.

"Nice," she cooed before swirling the head with her tongue then taking him slowly into her mouth inch-by-inch.

With a firm grip on his rigid shaft, her head and hand glided up and down in a smooth, piston-like motion. David, meanwhile, was in a state of shock. His eyes rolled up into the back of his head each time Brianna deep-throated his dick. The grip from her mouth and the swirling of her tongue were the stuff dreams were made of. The constant hum from inside her throat created vibrating sensations across his dick head that had him releasing tiny bursts of his creamy delight onto her tonsils.

"Mmm," she cooed while looking up into his eyes and teasing his head with her flicking tongue, "your dick tastes so good."
"Daaaaa-yum, Brianna," he gasped when he looked down into her sparkling eyes and watched her display.
"What, baby?" she asked while continuing to stroke his dick and plant soft kisses on its head.
"I wanna fuck you so bad."
"I know," she replied before deep-throating him once again. "I know you want me and I want you too. I've seen the way you've been watching me the past few weeks and I think it's *so* sexy."
"Really?" he asked, realizing that he had been busted.
"Yes, really. Did you bring condoms? I have some if you didn't."

David was on fire. It was if she had read his mind and was acting out the all scenes he had imagined. With his jogging pants hovering above his knees, David followed Brianna into the bedroom where he stood in awe while she undressed. Her tits were exquisite and her nipples were the biggest and roundest he had ever seen. His mouth watered at the thought of licking and sucking them. He was so wrapped up in watching her that he could barely remove his own clothes. By the time he pulled his shirt over his head, Brianna was laying in the bed, rubbing and squeezing her tits while smiling at him. With condoms in hand, David climbed into the bed and began kissing her cherry-flavored lips. His fingers probed her tight wet pussy, causing her to moan as they slid in and out of her.

"Not too rough, baby. It's been a while. I want that big juicy dick, baby," she moaned after taking his hand and slowly guiding his fingers in and out of her.

Struggling to maintain his composure, David slid the condom on and climbed atop of her. Her body shuddered when she felt the head of his dick sliding past her juicy lips. A moan escaped Brianna's mouth as her back arched and her candy cane-colored nails dug into his shoulders. She couldn't believe how hard his dick was or how big it felt. Though his strokes were uncomfortable at first, her juices surrounded his thrusting dick and smoothed his glide. Within moments, her body was moving in rhythm with his, her pussy taking every inch of him while her heels teased the backs of his tensed legs and thighs. Brianna could feel him fighting the urge to cum inside her, his dick rumbling as small blasts of cum escaped between each deep, penetrating thrust.

"Gimme that nut, David! Give it to me!" Brianna demanded, inspiring his strokes became deeper, harder, and faster.

Within seconds, wave after wave escaped his shaft spilling hot, creamy, nut from his cum-soaked sack. The continued in-and-out motion only added to the pleasure David was feeling. His only hope was that Brianna felt it too. He planted soft kisses on her quivering lips as they lay there in an orgasmic embrace. The smell of her body oil and the softness of her skin were making his dick hard again. Feeling that he had cum to quick anyway, David was determined to redeem himself. With slow deliberate strokes, he began to slide in and out, back and forth inside Brianna's still soaking-wet pussy.

As she lay there, she was awed by what she was feeling. Her body had barely recovered and yet here he was again, making her hotter and wetter with each stroke of his rapidly swelling dick. Somehow, he felt bigger and harder than before. She fought hard not to, but the moans kept escaping her mouth. Over and over she called his name as he dug deeper inside her. She could feel both his confidence and his intensity building with each passing moment. His pleasure became her delight as she kissed his lips and begged him to go even deeper. With her legs on his shoulders, David's dick was practically laying on her G-spot. Each stroke touched and teased it, causing her juices to rage like a waterfall. She gave up trying to count the number of times she had already climaxed.

David, meanwhile, was lost in a world all his own. This was the moment he had dreamed of, the moment he had fantasized about. He wasn't going to let it pass without leaving his mark. With one of Brianna's legs on his shoulder and the other resting on his thigh, David continued pounding her sweet pussy, looking into her glistening eyes while his thumb teased her swollen clit. Watching her squeeze and caress her massive tits was a turn-on all by itself, but when her tongue hit her right nipple, his senses went into overdrive. To him, a woman licking her own tit was the sexiest shit imaginable. He lowered her leg and resumed his position on top of her, sucking her tits one after the other while pounding her pussy.

"Fuck me, David, fuck me!" Brianna cried out as a rush of lava raced up his shaft.

The sensation of his dick jumping around inside her pussy caused her dam to break one more time, showering her lover with her own hot, creamy explosion. Unable to move and shaking with delight, David lowered his head onto Brianna's breasts and felt her gentle caress as she kissed him and whispered "Damn baby," over and over again in his ear.

Profile of a Virgin

For all intents and purposes, Adele was the closest thing to a virgin Chris had encountered since high school. Despite having had a child and a couple of lovers over the years, she had never experienced an orgasm. She knew little or nothing about receiving oral sex and had never given a blow job. Though anal sex was totally taboo, it wasn't necessarily out of the question. Even though she had been sheltered, Adele was at least open-minded. After weeks of hesitation, she finally revealed her desire for Chris to make love to her and show her what she had been missing. In the weeks that followed her revelation, Chris began referring to her as being "like a virgin."

Even though she hated it, Adele couldn't deny it. Neither her child's father nor the few men that she had been with since then had taught her anything about sex or making love beyond fulfilling their own sexual pleasures. She really didn't know what turned her on, or where or how she liked to be touched. She had heard about foreplay but never truly experienced it. She had even tried masturbation but didn't know enough about her own body to really enjoy it. To Adele, it was nothing more than lying there and playing with her own pussy.

At first, Chris was shocked by her explicit desires. After all, this woman was a grown-up version of the little girl he played with as a child. In fact, until junior high, they were convinced that they were cousins. When puberty set in, all that changed. His cute little playmate suddenly had a very adult-looking body. Although he still wanted to play, Chris was more interested in grown-up games.

Upon hearing her about Adele's plight, Chris found himself as interested as he was intrigued. The sexually explicit conversations he tried to engage her in were more like lectures. Not only was he literally teaching Adele about sex, but he was teaching her about her own body as well. Her ignorance was amusing to him, but made Adele very uncomfortable. A few times she became angry. Still, she was determined to see this through and was happy that Chris was being so patient with her. Though he was playing it cool, Chris was anything but patient. Their late-night phone conversations and sexting marathons only intensified his desire to have her. Often, the conversations became so intense that he found himself jacking off in the middle of the night just to relieve the anxiety. He had to have her. Ever since high school, he had dreamed of being Adele's first. College, relocations, relationships, and other factors got in their way though.

When he heard she was pregnant, Chris assumed she had gotten married and was living with her new family. When their paths crossed a few years later, he discovered that not much had changed. Adele was still as fine as cat hair, and despite having had a baby, she still had that gorgeous body that he remembered. She even had that same sweet shyness he loved so much.

After years of separation and weeks of frustrating anticipation here they were, alone in his dimly lit apartment listening to soft music. Unfortunately, the evening wasn't going quite the way he had planned. In fact, it was at a complete stand still. There she was dressed in a long denim skirt, a pink T-shirt with matching socks, a black and pink sweater and a pair of black crocs. Not only was this beautiful, chocolate-colored goddess dressed like an Amish housewife, Adele was also playing on her got-damned cell phone! Chris lost track of the time he spent listening to the constant beeps, bloops, dings, and pings that were coming from it. This was in no way what he had imagined their first night together would be like. After seriously contemplating scrapping the entire evening, he had a last-ditch moment of brilliance.

"I'm updating my profile," Adele replied after giggling at the goofiness of his text message.

"What did you post?"

"I posted that I was chilling with my homie Chris and that we were shooting the breeze and what not."

"Is that what people do on Facebook, sit around and post random personal information on their pages?"

"Pretty much," Adele replied while pecking away.

"How about I give you something to post?" he asked after standing up and walking over to the love seat.

"What would that be?" Adele asked, watching as he knelt by her knees.

"You'll see. Lift your ass," he commanded in a soft, smooth tone that was so seductive it made goose bumps rise all over her skin.

"Okay," she replied nervously before complying with his request.

Her eyes widened with shock and surprise when his warm hands crept slowly up her legs, under her skirt, and up her thighs all the way to her panties. With her ass still lifted, Chris pulled her white cotton panties down her soft, round thighs and over her shoes. She sat frozen, watching in amazement as her panties sailed across the room and landed on the floor by the entertainment center. Moments later, with Adele still speechless, Chris grabbed her by the waist and pulled her ass to the edge of the couch. Her heart threatened to leap out of her chest when he pushed her skirt up around her waist and placed her legs on his shoulders.

"Are you ready?" Chris asked, smiling while looking into her bewildered eyes.

"For what?" she gasped before his head disappeared between her quivering thighs.

The last time a man had his face this close to her 'privates' was six months ago at the doctor's office. Adele literally had no idea what was going to happen next.

"For this," he whispered before planting a soft wet kiss on her swollen clit.
"Oh…my…gawd!" she cried when his tongue began flicking across her bud, the curly black hairs around it becoming instantly saturated with a combination of saliva and her own juices. "Oh, shit Chris, *got-damn!*"

Adele's moans and feeble attempts to escape his grip were his ultimate turn-on. The more she tried to escape, the more intense his licking and sucking became. She didn't know whether she wanted to grab the back of his head to hold him in place, or push him away so that she could breathe. She even considered running the hell away! Her senses couldn't handle it. His lips on her body, his tongue on her clit, and his fingers sliding in and out of her creamy pussy were all driving Adele crazy. When his licking and sucking intensified even more, Adele abandoned her grip on the back of his head and began clutching the back of the couch. A wave of orgasmic pleasure flooded her abdomen before her milky rush showered Chris's tongue and lips. Beads of sweat formed all over her skin and made her clothes stick to her quivering body. When his face reappeared, his smiling lips were covered in her creamy glaze.

"What did you just do?" she gasped while sitting slumped down on the couch cushion with her head spinning.
"You didn't like it?" Chris asked after wiping his mouth with his shirt.
"Like it? I *loved* it!" Adele exclaimed, still trying to catch her breath.
"Good."
"What are you doing now?" she asked after his hands pushed her pink T-shirt up over her lacy white bra.
"What do you think I'm going to do?" Chris asked when he lifted her 36Cs out of their cups. "Damn, your tits are *so* fucking beautiful," he said while staring and shaking his head.

Kneeling between her legs once again, Chris squeezed Adele's soft round tits while his tongue circled and teased her hardened nipples. Chills began racing through her body all over again. A tingling sensation at the base of her spine threatened to bring tears to her eyes. His tongue was majestic! Chris was attacking her tits like a man possessed. His heavy breathing, the feel of his hands squeezing and massaging her tits while his tongue danced from nipple to nipple, and his aggression made Adele cum again and again. She could feel the hot cream pooling on the couch cushion below her round, naked ass. Before she could catch her breath, Chris had pulled her down onto the floor. She watched as he wrestled to slide a condom over his swollen dick head and down his shaft before sliding it inside her glistening pussy.

"Damn, Adele! Your pussy is so tight," Chris gasped as her creamy walls clamped onto and milked his dick like a vice.
"Your dick feels so big in my pussy!" she moaned while pulling his shirt up and kissing his chest.

Chris's thrusting dick wasted little time searching out and finding her G-spot, the one she didn't even know existed. With her eyes rolled up in the back of her head, Adele took him in. Her body had never known pleasure the way Chris was giving it. Though his dick wasn't the biggest she'd experienced, it was by far the best, and he knew how to work it too! With her legs on his shoulders, Chris pleasured her pussy for what seemed like an eternity. Adele had no idea that she could get this wet or that a dick could stay hard this long. The back of her skirt felt like a wet bath towel beneath her trembling ass. This was the feeling that she had heard about, talked about, dreamed about. It was damn worth the wait!

"Gimme dat pussy, Adele! Make me bust dis hard-ass nut!"

Faster and harder, deeper and stronger, Chris pounded Adele's pussy until she thought she was going to pass out. Suddenly, his dick began dancing around inside her, pulsating as wave after powerful wave of cum blasted from deep within his balls. After a few moments of holding him and kissing his lips, Adele released him so that he could relax next to her.

"What do you want me to do with this?" she asked, half out of breath when he handed her the phone.

"Since you like updating your profile so much, post what just happened."

"You think I won't?" she asked after opening her page and preparing to accept his challenge.

"Nope," he dared with a devilish grin.

"Thanks to Chris, I just had my first orgasm. Make that five," Adele read while pecking away on her iPhone screen. "He just fucked the shit out of me," she typed before laying her phone down on the floor next to her. "What do you want me to post next?"

"Well, let's see," Chris began as he lay on his back and Adele began planting soft kisses on his neck while stroking his limp dick.

"What are you doing?" she asked when she felt his hand gently nudging her head towards his lower extremities.

"Somebody wants to say hi to you."

"Wow! That was amazing!" Adele exclaimed when she saw Chris's dick go from limp to fully erect in a matter of seconds.

"Go ahead, say hi," he said after another gentle nudge.

"I don't know if I'll do it right."

"Just remember what I said. It's just like a popsicle."

"Okay," she replied, gripping his dick by its shaft and staring at it.

He waited patiently as Adele leaned in close, stroking his dick while studying it carefully. He wondered what was going through her mind, but he dared not ask because he didn't want to ruin the mood. The anticipation of her sucking his dick built even more when she leaned in slowly and planted one soft kiss after another on its throbbing head. His body shuddered when he felt Adele's tongue swirl his dick head for the first time. After several agonizing moments of her flicking tongue, Chris was treated to the pleasure of watching his dick disappear inside Adele's mouth. It felt better than he could have ever imagined! After a few adjustments to her gag reflex, she was taking in his entire dick. After holding it in place for a while, her head began bobbing slowly up and down on his dick while pumping his shaft with her clinched fist.

Chris couldn't believe what Adele was doing or how well she was doing it. For a woman who claimed she had never given a blow job, Adele was working his dick like a pro. She was doing it all: one hand...two hands...no hands! Kissing and sucking on his head while Chris stared, she even played with the pre-cum that had formed at the tip which made him lose control of his load. Before he could warn her, a flood of cream raced up through his shaft and exploded into Adele's hot wet mouth. But she didn't stop. Even as his cum spilled out and down his shaft, Adele kept stroking, sucking, and slurping. Out of breath, and suffering from temporary paralysis, Chris watched while Adele's pink tongue lapped up drops of spilled cum from her hand.

"Oh...my...damn!" he exclaimed.
That wasn't as bad as they said it was, she thought before licking his cream off her fingers and grabbing her phone. "Just gave head for the first time and judging by how hard Chris came, I did a great job," she typed before laying her phone back down.

Within seconds, her phone came alive with buzzes and alerts from her page.

"What do you suppose they're saying after reading your posts?"
"I don't care. I'm having fun," Adele replied with a smile as she lay at Chris's side and continued stroking his dripping dick. "What else would you like me to post?"
"Give me a few minutes and we'll see."

Twenty-five minutes later Adele made another post.

"I just had my titties and my ass fucked for the first time and I loved it!!!!"

Throughout the rest of the night, as their passionate and kinky sex-capade continued, Adele continued making posts about her night with Chris.

Naughty Thoughts

The thoughts I'm having about you right now are ones that shouldn't be shared.
They might change how you feel about me or make you a little scared.

Though I see you every day, your name is all I know.
I don't quite know what it is, but when I see you my lust starts to grow.

By the look that's etched across your face, it's clear you weren't ready for that.
We've come this far and since we're adults, I see no need to turn back.

Do I begin with your eyes and feline attraction of your soft sexy lips and their separate reaction?
Or what about your breasts so full inside that blouse? They'd feel great in my hands and better in my mouth.

I can see you have a question that is burning deep in your mind. The answer is yes!
I've already undressed you at least a hundred dozen times.

Your thighs and ass look soft and moist. Your body is so beautiful and stacked.
Just watching you walk here and there could give me a heart attack.

Why do you look so shocked as if you've never heard words such as these?
I'm sure someone has told you that your body is such a tease.

Don't look at me like that because I'm only telling you what's true.
What am I thinking right now? That's easy being deep inside of you.

I know our friendship is one thing, but I was a man before we met.
And as a man I can't help but think about making your body soft and wet.

The way your body moves is like a song that plays on the breeze.
Watching and wanting you like I do is making me weak in the knees.

I can hear your body calling like a phone that won't stop ringing.
The thought of being inside you has my whole damned body tingling.

Is it that I'm wearing you down? Do you suddenly like what I'm saying?"
At first you were ready to leave, but now it looks like you're staying.

The Upstairs Neighbor

The last thing that Pierce wanted to hear about was dating. Though it had been six months since his girlfriend of four years left, he still wasn't quite over it yet. In fact, part of him still hoped that she would return. His sister, Aileen, however, wasn't about to allow her baby brother to languish in misery over "that bitch," as Connie had come to be known. In an effort to jumpstart Pierce's love life, Aileen took it upon herself to introduce him to some of her single friends whom he quickly found fault with.

The first was April, who had four children by five different men. He discovered that the paternity of her youngest was actively up for debate. Next was Yolaunda, the pothead. Besides chain-smoking cigarillos and blunts, she was a workaholic who rarely had time for anything beyond sleeping and getting high. Though the sex was off the chain, her character lacked substance and as a result left way too much to be desired. Last, there was Stacey, the delusional gold digger. She was very up front and quickly made her desires to be spoiled and pampered known. On their first and last date, she quizzed Pierce about everything from his annual earnings, his 401K, and his five-year plan to his credit rating and net worth. She turned her nose up at her Pierce's one-year-old, fully loaded Nissan Altima and his spacious, two-bedroom "Bachelor Pad." She told him he needed to "step his game up." Meanwhile, she lived in a cramped "studio" apartment with rented furniture and drove a two-year-old BMW 3 series that she could barely afford the payments on. But Aileen, being the loving and concerned sister that she was, "vowed" not to give up until and Pierce got out of his rut.

Bored and in need of a laugh, Pierce decided to stop by the liquor store and purchase everything he needed to make his famous margaritas. Being that it was a midsummer Friday night, a few iced-down pitchers were just what the doctor ordered. Around 9:30 p.m. and well into their third pitcher, Pierce, Aileen, and her husband Mike sat on the front porch of her two-family apartment building drinking, laughing, and fighting mosquitoes. Their fun was suddenly interrupted by the sounds of thumping base and a raged exhaust. Seconds later, a green, late-nineties Cadillac STS rumbled to a stop in front of them. The first person out of the sedan was a dark-skinned, plus-sized woman with bright red hair and a body-hugging dress that looked about three sizes too small.

"Who in the hell is that?" Pierce asked while filling his glass
"That's my neighbor Michelle. She's cool, but as you can see she's a little ghetto."
"Just a little?" Mike scoffed while lighting a Newport.
"Damn, that's a banging-ass Nissan. I wonder whose it is."
"It's mine," Pierce replied before sitting back down. "Do you like it?"
"Hell yeah," Michelle replied emphatically while inspecting the chrome twenties on his ride.

As soon as the song ended, the passenger-side door opened and out she stepped. This five-foot something, brick shit house was the finest sista Pierce had ever laid eyes on. She had the face of and angel, but her body was made for sin! Her white wife beater was stretched tightly over her bodacious melons while a pair of cut-off jean shorts hugged her voluptuous thighs and round ass like a glove. Her micro braids were pulled back in a ponytail which gave him a better glimpse of her beautiful, round, dark chocolate-colored face. When he saw her, Pierce almost dropped his cup.

"Got damn!" he exclaimed, causing Mike to burst into a fit of laughter. "That's Michelle's daughter, Michelle. I know, ghetto, right?" Aileen quipped while shaking her head at the Altima's gawkers.

"Babe, I don't think your brother gives a rat's ass about your issues with their names. I bet he doesn't even remember Connie's name right now."

"Connie who?" Pierce asked with a grin before sitting his cup on the porch and sailing down the steps en route to the sidewalk.

"Momma, whose car are you staring at?"

"It's mine," Pierce interrupted smoothly. "Sorry, I didn't mean to be so rude. I'm Pierce, Aileen's brother."

"I'm Michelle," she replied, smiling while taking his extended hand.

"Wanna go for a ride?"

"I don't know. I mean I…"

"Girl, you betta go for a ride with this fine young nigga. If you don't, I damn sho' will," her mother declared, causing a massive lump to form in Pierce's throat.

"Not tonight. I mean, I have plans tonight. Some other time, maybe?" she asked while gazing into his glassy eyes.

"That's cool," Pierce replied before releasing her hand and trying not to stare at her tits.

The next afternoon after working half-a-day, Pierce sat on his couch half asleep while listening to music and enjoying the cool air conditioning. He had just dozed off when suddenly, his phone began buzzing. When he looked at it, he saw a text message from an unknown number. Although he didn't recognize it, he smiled when he read the message.

"This is Michelle. I got your number from your sister. I wanna get with you later. If it's cool, hit me up."

Feeling himself suddenly come alive again, Pierce immediately called her back.

"Hello?"

"Hi, Michelle, it's Pierce."

"I know who it is, boo. Whuz crackin?"

"Not a whole lot, just trying to beat this heat. Whassup with you?"

"Shit. I wanted to see if you wanted to hook up tonight."

"That's cool. What would you like to get into?" he asked while imagining her standing in front of him dancing naked.

"It doesn't matter as long as it's inside, boo. It's hot as hell out there today."

"I feel you. What time should I pick you up?"

"Is 9:30 cool?" she asked eagerly.

"No doubt, see you later."

"Bye, cutie," she cooed before hanging up the phone.

Before his phone hit the coffee table, Pierce was thinking of all the positions he could put Michelle in later. With that big round ass and curvaceous hips, doggy style was a must! His mouth watered at the thought of his tongue circling and swirling all over her nipples. Pierce spent the next couple of hours making sure his place was spotless. He swept and mopped the kitchen and bathroom, cleaned the tub and shower, washed and put away the dishes, and dusted all his furniture. Next, he changed the sheets on the bed and vacuumed all the carpets. Finally, he went through the closet looking for something to wear before deciding that simplicity was the best course of action. Besides, he didn't want his intentions to seem too obvious. After taking a long hot shower, he put on a white Coogi shirt and matching athletic shorts. Afterwards, he searched through his selection of colognes before selecting his favorite, Burberry. Pierce also made sure that the condoms were on the nightstand, behind the lamp and out of sight but well within reach. He also put some in the living room under the couch cushion just in case they didn't make it to the bedroom. After a couple of spot checks, the scene was set. Tonight, he was going to wax that chocolate ass.

When Pierce arrived at 9:15, part of him hoped that Aileen wouldn't see him. Even though she had given Michelle his number, he knew that she wasn't up to his sister's standards. Still, there was something sexy about Michelle's "hood" attitude. The tone of her voice, the shape of her body and her whole demeanor made Pierce want to fuck the shit out of her on sight. After a brief moment of contemplation, he stopped caring what his sister thought and stepped out of his car. There on the porch as he walked up the stairs were Michelle, her mother, and Aileen. They were polishing off last night's leftover pitcher.

A good sign, Pierce thought when Michelle took her cup to the head.

"You ready to bounce, boo?" she asked after placing her cup on the table.

"Ummm...sure," he replied, caught off guard but thrilled that she was so eager.

"Good 'cause these margaritas got me hot and hungry."

"No problem," he replied with a smile. "Whassup up, sis?"

"Just chillin'."

"Y'all have a good time," Michelle's mother called out with a smile while filling her cup.

"Yes ma'am, we will," Pierce replied when Michelle passed in front of him on the way to the car. *If she only knew how much fun I'm going to have,* he thought when he glanced at her daughter's voluptuous ass.

"What sounds good to eat?" he asked when he opened Michelle's door and watched her settle in.

Her tight jean shorts, low-cut blouse, and fragrant perfume had his dick throbbing in his shorts.

"I don't know," she replied while adjusting her shorts which had ridden up her dark, Godiva-smooth thighs.

"What sounds good to you?" she asked when he got in.

"Honestly?" he asked while smiling and staring into her glassy eyes.

"Yeah."

"You."

"Damn, P. It's like that?" she asked, the sound of his voice making her nipples stand up and demand attention.

"Yes, it is," he replied with a wink before driving off.

A short while later after picking up a pizza and some wings, they arrived at Pierce's apartment. The entire place smelled of black cherry thanks to the candles that he had left burning. Best of all, it was nice and cool.

"Oh, you was tryin' to set the mood, huh?" Michelle quipped after taking in her surroundings.

Under normal circumstances, she would have thought he was either gay or lived with a woman because Pierce's place was immaculate. Nothing was out of place. All the furniture and décor were color-coordinated. A large, black ceramic panther with green eyes loomed in a makeshift jungle composed of artificial plants. Michelle even heard soft music coming from the rear of the apartment, and judging by the ambiance, she quickly concluded that the music must be coming from the bedroom. His manhood was quickly redeemed by the entertainment center with the obligatory, large flat-screen television, high-definition surround-sound stereo, and PlayStation 3 with controllers on the floor in front of it.

A true bachelor, she thought as he carried the food into the dining room. "I can't eat too much of that. Everything I eat settles in my titties and my ass."
"You won't hear me complaining."
"I bet I won't," she replied a wink.

After dinner and a couple more margaritas, Pierce and Michelle sat on the couch enjoying the soothing sounds of Sade while making funny small talk. Sitting with her feet on the couch and leaning on Pierce's thigh gave him the perfect view of her sumptuous bust line. He had to adjust his shirt a few times so that she wouldn't get an accidental poke from the tent that had risen. He also found himself fighting the urge to grab Michelle's tits which kept calling him through the navy-blue T-shirt she was wearing. It didn't help that her perfume was lingering in his nose, further fueling his desire to fuck her right there on the couch. Pretending to let his arm slip, he groped her tits with a light sweep of his hand.

"My bad," he said, slightly amused by his own childish antics.

"For real, P?" Michelle quipped when she sat up and faced him. "We're both too old for that kind of shit. That was a high school move and I don't know about you, but I'm grown."

"Meaning?"

"Meaning," she began before pulling her shirt out of her shorts and lifting it over her head, "if you wanna touch my tits or anything else, don't bullshit. Just do it. If I ain't feeling it, I'll let you know."

"Are you feeling it now?"

"What do you think?" she asked after unhooking her bra and letting it slide down her arms.

Pierce was mesmerized by her perfectly formed tits. Her nipples were hard and begging to be sucked. The combination of what he was seeing and her smooth, bold delivery sent his senses into sexual overload. Before he could gather his senses, Pierce had Michelle down on the couch with her tits in his mouth.

"Damn, P!" she gasped as he attacked her nipples one after the other.

His passionate grunts, aggressive sucking, and heavy breathing had her clit throbbing against her red satin G-string. The grip from his mouth and hands on her tits combined with the tequila had her panties soaked. Michelle's legs snaked their way around Pierce's waist as he lay on top of her, feasting on her melons while grinding his dick against her.

"Bite that titty baby," she cooed when she felt his teeth graze her tender flesh. "Shit baby, sit back for a minute."

When he sat up, Michelle sprung up off the couch and stood directly in front of him. The glowing candlelight across the room accentuated her voluptuous silhouette. She made a deliberate show of slowly undoing her shorts and peeling them away from her luscious hips and ass. When they hit the floor, she stepped out of them and straddled Pierce's lap.

"Can you handle all this woman, baby?" she asked while grinding her clit back and forth against his throbbing dick.

"Hell, yeah!" he declared before grabbing her ass and pulling her closer so that he could resume his feast.

Gripping the back of the couch with one hand and Pierce's head with the other, Michelle continued her grinding. The sensation of riding him not only made her juices soak through her panties but the front of his shorts as well.

"I need you inside me now, P!" Michelle gasped when she felt an orgasm looming.

"Get down on the floor, baby, and let me hit that pussy from behind."

"Okay, sexy," she said before passionately kissing his lips and standing up.

"No, baby, keep that thong on," he said when she reached for her waistband.

"Okay, daddy. Damn u freaky," she said with a grin before settling on the floor in front of him.

Seconds later, Pierce was kneeling behind her and admiring her round, juicy ass. After sliding his rubber on, he slid the red G-string to the side and teased her clit with his finger before sliding it in her pussy. After a few minutes of finger play, he replaced it with his swollen dick. Michelle's pussy was the wettest and tightest he'd ever felt. He slid back and forth a few times, pressing a little harder with each stroke of his dick head against her soft, quivering lips. Michelle's nails dug into the carpet when she felt his swollen head finally penetrating her sugar walls. Her back arched as a moan after moan escaped her mouth. Though she had already taken inch after inch, Michelle thought she could still feel his dick going deeper and deeper inside her while her walls stretched around him.

"Damn, yo dick is big! Fuck me, daddy. Pound this pussy like you want to!" Michelle gasped when she felt his balls slapping against her clit.

And pound it he did stroke after stroke, thrust after thrust. The sight of sweat beads forming on her chocolate ass and the way it jiggled made Pierce fuck her that much harder. The sounds of Michelle's voice and her tight grip on his dick had brother man lost in the moment. Her moans, her heavy breathing, and the sound of his name escaping her lips were all he could hear, like lyrics being sung over the soft instrumental playing in the background. With his fingers on her thighs and his thumbs spreading her ass, Pierce found his eyes fixated on the puckered brown eye buried deep within her cheeks. The thought of that red string buried deep in her ass had his mind racing. He wondered if she had ever taken a dick in the ass or if his would even fit inside. With each stroke, moan, and occasional smack of her ass, his curiosity grew more intense.

Remembering what she had told him on the couch, Pierce decided to see if she was "feeling" him. After sucking his thumb for a few seconds, he laid it on Michelle's puckered asshole and began swirling and massaging it in a soft circular motion. After several moments of moaning, pussy pounding, and ass teasing, he applied just enough pressure for his thumb to slide inside. By her reaction, it was clear that her ass was enjoying every second of it. Gripping the carpet with one hand and Pierce's thigh with the other, Michelle threw her pussy hard against his thrusting dick and sliding thumb. Wave after wave of cum blasted around his dick, making her pussy voice its delight while her juices drenched and dripped from his balls.

"You got this pussy talkin', daddy! Shit daddy, *shit*!" she gasped as his balls continued slapping her clit.

"Turn over, sexy," he whispered before licking her on the spine just above her round, chocolate ass.

As soon as her back hit the floor, Pierce was on top with his dick thrusting hard and fast inside her pussy. When their lips met, Michelle's tongue was inside his mouth almost instantly. Her nails dug into his shoulders the second his mouth locked onto the side of her neck. The feel of his balls smacking against her ass made her back arch and her eyes tear up with delight. Pierce had discovered a secret that she no doubt intended to hide. Michelle's ass was her "hot spot" and he had touched and teased it to the point that she almost lost control. His hard, fast thrusting was making her big tits bounce in his face. Pierce loved every second of it too. She almost lost her mind when he lifted her right leg onto his shoulder. No man had ever been this deep in her pussy nor made her cum so hard and so often. It was if he had a road map to her G-spot and was hitting it with every stroke.

"Lay yo ass down!" Michelle demanded when he lowered her quivering leg.

Within seconds she was on top, sliding up and down his pole and bouncing her big round ass on him.

With his hands pressed to the floor and her tits dangling above his lips, Michelle took total control of Pierce's dick. She wasn't going to be outdone by him fucking the shit out of her. She was going to fuck him better than any bitch ever had.

"Damn, baby, take that dick!" he cried, making her bounce harder and faster.
"Whose dick is this? Whose dick is this?" she demanded when she felt him swelling and getting ready to explode.
"It's yours! Got *damn*, it's yours!" Pierce surrendered before unleashing a torrent of cum inside her that was so hard it made him light-headed.

As they lay on the floor panting and sweating, they giggled thinking that the neighbors had heard everything. But neither of them cared because, frankly, it was too good to. They had thrown caution to the wind and found the path to ecstasy as a result. As they shared kiss after passionate kiss, they were happy that fate had brought them together. Their bodies writhed in anticipation of the next time they would let themselves go. In the back of his mind, Pierce knew that it was only a matter of time before he was literally deep inside her chocolate ass. In her mind, Michelle knew that it was only a matter of time before she let him.

Alex and Tisha

From the upcoming novel *Operation Cover-up: Rise of the Black Mamba*
By P D Baldwin

Gusting, gale force winds swirled around the penthouse while pelting its windows with tiny hail stones and hard, driving rains. The relentless crash of icy waters on the patio was reminiscent of drums beating in the distance. The storm outside had been raging for hours, but it was nothing compared to the passionate storm raging atop the California King. Their body heat was so intense that it was causing the master suite's smoked windows to fog up. With candles burning brightly on each nightstand and flashes of lightening outside, he had the best possible glimpses of her beauty. He was not sure if it was the sexy way she bit her lip when his name tried escaping her mouth, the tears of ecstasy that rolled down her Hershey-colored cheeks, or the sensual way she cupped her breasts while arching her back. Whatever it was, it was fueling his desire to keep thrusting his dick deep inside her while devouring her hardened nipples.

"Alex!" she gasped when another climax erupted from deep within her abdomen.

His name escaped her mouth two more times as she sat perched on his lap with her creamy walls pulsating and milking his dick with each up and down glide of her soft, round hips.

"Tell me you love me," she pleaded while pinning his hands to the bed and thrusting her pelvis to his.

She needed to hear him say it. She needed to hear his words. She needed to know that this moment was real. Nothing else mattered, not even the buzzing that was vibrating the nightstand to their right.

"I love you, Tisha," he whispered while staring into her eyes.

The next orgasm sent rapid-fire shudders of orgasmic electricity up and down her spine. While riding this wave of pleasure, she collapsed onto his chest. When her lips met his, Alex's tongue began probing the depths of her mouth. He repeatedly inhaled her passionate moans, while gripping her ass and thrusting his dick upwards into her pussy.

"Shit baby, *shit!*" Tisha cried as another orgasm erupted which sent her G-spot into a pulsating frenzy of delight.

Was this her fifth or ninth orgasm? Tisha was so engulfed in Alex's pleasure that she had lost count of them. It didn't matter though because her body was his to command. His every touch, kiss, and caress sent chills coursing through her body all the way to her soul. No man, not even her husband could ever make her feel the way Alex did. She belonged to him; mind, body, and soul. As she bounced up and down on his thrusting dick, her soft green eyes rained tears of ecstasy down her soft cheeks and onto her breasts. Her ivory and gold manicured nails raked his arms and chest when she sat back up, causing tiny, crimson-streaked cuts to appear on his flesh.

When her back hit the black satin sheets, Tisha knew that her pleasure ride was not over just yet. The look on Alex's face was *so* intense, *so* sexy. His deep, purposeful thrusts were honing in on her G spot like missiles. Harder, deeper, and faster he pounded her pussy with stroke-after-stroke from his swollen dick. Not content to just lie there and take it, Tisha tried matching his thrusts with her own. Each rise and fall of her hips sent streams of her juices spilling down the crack of her ass. The intense euphoria of their love making had her ready to faint, but she did not.

With her legs high atop his shoulders, Tisha delighted in each plunge of his dick. Seconds became minutes and minutes became hours as he pleasured her over and over from various angles and in multiple positions.

"You love this pussy, don't you, Alex?" Tisha gasped when she felt him swelling and pressing hard against her sugar walls. "Show me, Alex! FUCK ME!" she demanded while grabbing his hips and thrusting her pussy hard against his dick.

The sensation of his sack banging the crack of her ass while his tongue circled her nipples made the back of her head want to explode. As his relentless pounding continued, creamy juices rained down from her flower and pooled beneath her quivering ass. She wanted Alex in every way possible, even if it meant surrendering her tender, virgin asshole which only his thumbs had invaded thus far. Whatever he wanted, Tisha did not mind because this was her man, and she was willing to do whatever it took to please him.

Now Alex was behind her and with his hands locked onto her waist, he was feeding Tisha all-of-the dick she could take. The ripples across her chocolate-colored ass intensified his desire to leave his mark on this sexy vixen. He cupped her left breast and gently massaged her nipple while leaning down and kissing her tattooed shoulder. Her back arched when his hot, wet tongue teased her spine. His touch, his power, and his passion were perfection. As another orgasm hit and her body felt weak, Tisha thought about tapping out. For whatever the reason, Alex seemed more energetic than normal. No matter what she tried, he could not seem to get enough. There was pleasure in the pain that she was feeling, and because of that, Tisha was not about to throw in the towel just yet. She prayed silently that it would not end; that he would continue to ignore the intrusions from the nightstand while taking her body to new heights of ecstasy.

"Damn, Alex, *shit!*" she cried when she heard his primal cries.

The gush of cum from his thrusting dick caused her dam to break simultaneously. Flashes of lightening brightened the bedroom once again as Alex's head snapped back and he howled toward the heavens, like a wolf atop a mountain's peak. His long, ebony hair rested on his chiseled, caramel-colored shoulders while cum erupted from his dick like an orgasmic volcano. He repeatedly smacked her ass as she thrust against him with her sugar walls milking him of every ounce of cum. With one last thrust of his dick, Tisha collapsed onto the bed and buried her face in the pillow. As she lay there quivering, Alex was positive he heard the sheets ripping.

He lay down beside Tisha and watched her body's reactions. He was pleased with his performance, especially when her tiny fists slowly released the shredded fibers that were intertwined between her fingers. While she laid face-down on her pillow still trembling and shivering, his tongue traced the length of her spine from her neck to the crack of her round ass. After a few trips up and down her back, Alex lay back down and let his fingers trace the same journey. They continued their journey beyond the base of her spine, through the valley of her ass where they gently teased her puckered hole. Moaning and writhing in an orgasmic frenzy, Tisha grabbed his wrist before his middle finger went too deep. Seconds later, his wayward fingers settled between the lips of her dripping pussy. His middle finger touched and teased her pulsating clitoris, causing her thighs to shudder before finally locking on his hand.

"Why…are…you…teasing…me…like…that?"
"Because you like it so much," he replied in a voice that made her body cry out for his tender kiss.

After leaning down, he repeatedly obliged her shoulder with his lips while making small wet circles with the tip of his tongue.

"You better quit that shit, Alex. You know that's my spot," she cooed while willing her body to relax.
One of many," he whispered before lying down next to her.

After making sure that he was comfortable, Tisha laid her head on his chest and began running her fingers over his tattooed abs. Chills coursed through her body when she closed her eyes and allowed her fingertips to read his body like a brail board. Her hand continued its descent until she reached his dripping, semi-erect manhood. Slowly, she caressed and stoked it, feeling it expand in her hand while circling his cum-soaked head with her thumb. While stroking his shaft, she placed soft, wet kisses on his body, beginning at his shoulder and moving down his chest to his stomach, and finally to his waistline. Alex shuddered when he felt Tisha's soft lips and wet tongue gently kissing his swollen head. Her strokes became shorter and slower while taking inch-after-inch into her hot, wet mouth. His whole body shook with delight when she began repeatedly deep-throating his dick before looking into his glassy eyes.

"You like that, don't you, daddy?" Tisha asked before her pink tongue continued its dance on his dick head.

Her stroking hand and flicking tongue made it impossible for Alex to speak. Much to her delight, he gently palmed the back of her head while thrusting his dick slowly in out of her tight mouth. The sensation of him gently banging the back of her throat and swelling between her puckered lips had Tisha's juices running down the insides of her thighs. Alex's pleasure was her weakness. She knew head was his weakness and without a doubt, Tisha was a "head master." His moans and the way he called her name were *so* sexy.

"Tisha! Damn! Damn! *Damn!*"

Her hand and mouth glided up and down his shaft in unison, increasing speed and pressure with each stroke. Alex tried to hold it back but couldn't. Tisha's intensity had him coating the back of her throat with the blasts of sweet pre-cum. Though she hated the taste, she felt some vindication from making him writhe in passionate agony. After all, Tisha was so accustomed to his sexual dominance that she was determined to turn the tables on him whenever she could. She repressed her gag reflex the deeper she took him in, being careful to exhale and send shudders across his thrusting head. Sensing his eminent explosion, Tisha pulled him out of her mouth and watched the fireworks.

"Hello!" she laughed when his thick, white cum arced from his head and landed on her pumping hand.

"Why'd you move?" Alex gasped with hints of both satisfaction and disappointment in his voice.

"You know I don't like the taste of that shit, Alex. And besides, you're not my husband, remember? And why didn't you use the flavored condoms I brought? You know I hate the taste of latex and that lubricant makes my mouth numb."

"Sorry Tish, but given the circumstances, I couldn't find that specific condom. And correct me if I'm wrong, but weren't you just in control of this?"

"But…"

"That's what I thought," he interrupted sarcastically. "Now wash your hands and go to sleep."

"Fuck you, Alex."

Later that morning, Tisha awoke and found herself alone in his bed. She struggled to get her bearings while looking for the source of that incessant buzzing. Her Blackberry lay on the nightstand just beyond an empty bottle of Paul Masson and two overturned glasses. She picked it up and cringed when she saw the ugly face on the screen. After quickly looking around the room, she pressed the *send* button.

"Hello?"

"Weh a yu?" barked an angry, thick West Indian accent. "Mi a call all night!"

"I got tired and had to…"

"Cha? Naa badda mi wit dat shit !" he fired back angrily. "I an da clock and yu fuckin' it up for mi. Move yu backside! Undastan, Tisha girl?"

"Yes honey. I'm…"
"Click."

The phone went dead before she could say *"sorry."* After taking a deep breath, she stepped out of the bed and on to the plush beige carpet. Though logs still burned in the fireplace, the room seemed much cooler than before. She picked Alex's shirt up off the floor and put it on, becoming instantly intoxicated by the scent of his Burberry cologne. She walked through the bedroom's French doors and through a short corridor leading to a massive living room. Even though it was the middle of the day, the penthouse was still rather dark because custom blinds were mounted over the smoked glass at all the windows and the patio doors. Tisha smiled to herself when she saw their clothes and shoes strewn carelessly about the living and dining rooms. Now standing by the black leather sofa, she looked to see if she could see or hear him anywhere.

"Alex? Alex? Asshole," Tisha sighed finally before picking her black lace thong up off the smoked glass and brass coffee table.

She walked through the living room and passed the nook that lead into the kitchen. She was instantly frozen by the scene inside the wall's built in aquarium. The blue light cast an eerie haze over the rapid movements behind its smoked glass. *Yuck,* she thought while watching their scaly, leathery bodies coil and contract. Tisha regained her composure and continued into the kitchen, which like the most of the penthouse was decorated in black, marble, and polished chrome. She grabbed a rocks glass off the counter and walked to the massive refrigerator. The bright light illuminated the dark rooms and bathed her shapely silhouette as she stood in front of its open doors. The cool air hardened her dark, round nipples which poked through his shirt like daggers. After pouring some orange juice, she closed the doors only to drop the glass on the floor.

"Got-dammit, Alex!" she cried while clutching her heart and shaking frantically.

Meanwhile, he stood quietly there silently watching her through the strands of hair that were matted to his head. For a split-second, her eyes feasted on the masterpiece in front her; a sexy, chiseled, and tattooed, body standing there glistening while he gripped the white towel that was draped around his broad shoulders.

"Why-the-fuck-are you always sneaking up on me? You're worse than…"
"Simon?" he interrupted sarcastically.
"No, Alex, a fucking cop."
"Well, we both know I'm not a cop," he replied before squatting to retrieve the glass and wipe up the spill.
"Kiss my foot while you're down there," she said before lifting her juice splashed leg and foot towards his mouth.

He glanced lustfully at her rose-tattooed foot and the vine that wrapped around her leg and up her creamy thigh before disappearing under his shirt.

"You'd like that too much," he replied in a low, raspy voice while standing in front of her gazing down into her green eyes.

Alex's bedroom eyes and smooth voice were her weakness and it was beginning to show. Even though she was on borrowed time, looking into his hazel eyes, smelling his cologne, and seeing the sweat on his half-naked body made Tisha ache for his touch. Her body was begging to be taken right there on the floor. The electricity Alex was emitting was filling her panties with her own creamy juices. Her knees began to buckle when he leaned in closer, the heat from his body damn near melting hers.

"I have to go," she said softly with his lips hovering ever so close to hers.
"I know."
"It won't always be like this," she whispered with her voice cracking and tears forming in the corners of her eyes.

Meanwhile, Alex stood emotionless. Even when Tisha buried her face in his chest and began to sob out loud, he never made a move. Though his first impulse was to push her away, he knew he couldn't; not yet anyway.

"Please don't ever leave me, Alex," she pleaded while hugging him tightly. "I won't," he surrendered before wrapping his arms around her.

Tokyo, Japan

In the luxurious penthouse suite of the Kadoyu hotel, a petite, shapely young woman was pacing nervously near the balcony door. The wind gently kissed her blonde-streaked hair as it lay on her caramel-colored shoulders. Her shear, spaghetti-strapped nightgown, matching bra, and see through panties clung closely to her body and hugged her curvaceous frame like gloves.

"Relax, Lexi," interrupted the voice from her hidden earpiece, "You're gonna be fine."
"Easy for you to say, Ko," she replied nervously. "A Yakuza boss isn't planning on drugging and raping you."
"And he won't be doing that to you either. Follow the plan to the letter and you'll be out of there before you know it. Besides, I'm right here to bail you out if you get jammed up."
Meanwhile outside the lobby, a stretched Maybach limousine crept to a stop underneath the hotel's burgundy and gold canopy. Two men, one tall and young and one shorter and older, exited the rear before the nervous driver could open the door. Both men were dressed in black, Armani suits, black patent-leather Cole Haans, and dark glasses. The shorter of the men had gray, tapered haired that was oiled and brushed to the back. As they entered the hotel lobby, his young counterpart quickly concluded a conversation on his cell phone.

"The Jamaican has guaranteed the security and delivery of our shipments. He has also proven able to expedite them when necessary while maintaining an exceptional level of purity. I suggest we…"

"Quiet, Ryugi," demanded the older man while waving his hand. "Is she here?"

"Yes she is, sir," Ryugi responded half-heartedly.

"Show me!"

Although annoyed by the request, Ryugi reluctantly complied. After scrolling through his messages, he held his Cell phone out for the old man to see. On the screen was a picture of the same young woman who was pacing upstairs. He scrolled through several more pictures much to the old man's delight. Each shot was of her in a different outfit and sensual poses.

"She is exquisite. Does she have a nice booty?" he asked before pulling a pill bottle from his inner blazer pocket. "

"Mr. Nakamura, this is hardly the time to be…"

"Silence, Ryugi!" he demanded again. "A man such as myself is entitled to an occasional indulgence and this just happens to be one of them. Any other affairs can wait until morning. Now, bring me to her and hold all my calls."

During the elevator ride to the top floor, Boss Nakamura quickly downed two of the blue pills before taking a sip from the silver flask that was in his other pocket.

Meanwhile in the suite, Lexi continued pacing nervously while waiting for her suitor to arrive.

"Lexi, I'm with you every step of the way so listen to me carefully. His routine is exactly the same. Avoid the cognac because it's laced. If he offers you a drink, request bottled water. I switched it out earlier. He's very quick with syringes. He keeps them in his pocket and they're full of a sedative. He drugs his victim up then rapes her, before tossing her to his bodyguards."

"You witnessed this, Ko?" she asked nervously.

"I've been watching this sick fuck for the past six months, Lexi. This is his routine. He has many strange fetishes and one of them is rap video vixens. He's gonna ask you to do something to take your mind off him like dancing, stripping, or making a drink. That's where I come in. I'll be watching his every move. If you slip, I'll put one in his eye. You got all that?"

"Sorry, Ko but I can't help being nervous. I'm just not used to being this close to a target, and Alex would go ballistic if he knew I was this close to Boss Nakamura."

"I know but Alex is handling the N.Y. job, and Karma wasn't available, remember? So relax 'cause I got your back. And um…by the way."

"Yes, Ko?" she asked while nervously rubbing her hands together.

"I love that um…uniform."

"Ko Hinomura, are you flirting with me when you are supposed to be watching my back?"

"Trust me, Lexi. I'm watching your back and your front," he mused while admiring her body through the scope of his high-powered, Mk-11 sniper rifle.

"Alex would whup that ass if he heard you talking to me like that."

"Well, he's not here now, is he?"

"I guess not," she replied while standing in front of the door and winking at him.

At that moment, the door of the suite swung open, and in the doorway, were Boss Nakamura and Ryugi. Lexi watched in silent disgust as the two men ogled her while whispering and smiling. After a vigorous hand shake, Boss Nakamura nodded to Ryugi before patting him on the back and closing the door behind him.

Showtime, she thought before casually stepping away from the balcony door.

"He just promised you to the head bodyguard. It's time to go into Jinx mode."

"That shit ain't happening, Ko," she whispered as Boss Nakamura stood there salivating.

Even though she had every reason to be afraid, Lexi was as cool as a cucumber. With a smile on her face and the wind at her back, she silently recited everything Ko had told her. Tonight she was going to be a video vixen for Boss Nakamura. Tonight, if only for a brief moment, she was going to fulfill his every erotic fantasy. By the time he stopped staring and began his approach, Lexi had already settled into character.

His handsome appearance and charm aside, Boss Nakamura was the lowest form of life imaginable. In addition to being a one of the most powerful gangsters in all of Asia, he was a sadist and a rapist. During his tenure with the Yakuza, he had either ordered or participated in the murder of over 200 men, women, and children. His greatest pleasure however, was sexually degrading women. Rape and torture were among his favorite tools. Now, Lexi was alone in a room with him and her mission was to kill him.

"You look *so* beautiful. How many videos have you danced in?"
"Too many to count," she said softly before teasing her fingertip with her tongue.
"Damn," Ko thought while eyeing her body like a lion stalking a gazelle.

Her breasts were round and firm. Her flat stomach flowed smoothly down into her round hips, and her ass was exquisite: round, smooth, and very enticing. A perfectly-timed breeze came thru the balcony door blowing her gown against her skin, hardening her nipples.

"Would you like a drink?" Boss Nakamura asked after becoming noticeably aroused.
"How about you relax while I fix you a drink instead, you sexy hunk-of-a man?"
"Vodka and tonic with a twist of lime, please," he replied giddily.
"Make yourself comfortable, Mr. Nakamura," she cooed with her hips swaying side-to-side as she walked to the bar.
"This is your chance, Lexi."

Her every movement was sexually exaggerated for Boss Nakamura, hypnotizing and mesmerizing him the longer he watched, and she made sure to keep him in her line of sight. While watching her, both Ko and Boss Nakamura secretly fantasized about the things that they would love to do to and with her body. Even though his mission was to protect her, Lexi's angelic voice and seductive demeanor were making Ko lose his focus. The longer Boss Nakamura ogled her, the more jealous he became. At one point, Ko had his head in the crosshairs of his scope and his finger on the trigger.

After a brief session of dancing and teasing, Lexi selected a rocks glass from the bar and filled it with ice. She looked over her right shoulder to see what Boss Nakamura was doing, and not surprisingly, he was undressing. For a man in his sixties, he was in pretty good physical shape. His body was tattooed with an exquisite green, yellow, and black dragon.

"Your tattoo is beautiful. Does it mean something?" Lexi asked while secretly wishing she could kill his bodyguard as well.
"It means I am a very powerful man," Nakamura replied with a huge, sinister grin.

With a smile on her face and a not-so-subtle swing in her hips, Lexi continued teasing her target by gently squeezing and massaging her right breast. Her smile and his lust-filled hypnosis made Boss Nakamura miss the stealthy removal of a vial from her bra. after she turned around, Lexi quickly opened it and dumped it into his drink. When she turned around to face him again, she had the drink in one hand and the lime in the other. While slowly walking towards him, she dropped lime twist in the glass and licked its juice from her fingers. She was amazed at how quickly Boss Nakamura snatched the glass and to her surprise, gulped it down; lime twist and all.

"I love American rap music. Will you shake your booty for me?"
"Anything for you, cutie," she replied, not surprised but disgusted all the same.

Lexi watched as he reached into the nightstand, pulled out a remote, and activated the stereo across the room. The thumping base and suggestive lyrics made her character even more seductive. Without any provocation, her body began to sway rhythmically to the beat. She cupped her breasts while gyrated sensually; her hands instantly becoming her lover's hands. Sweat began pouring from Nakamura's brow when she dipped it low and brought it back up slow. As soon as she smacked her own ass, his heart started racing. With his hands shaking, and his vision blurring, Boss Nakamura reached into his blazer pocket and pulled out a small platinum case.

"He's going for the syringes."

Even though his senses and motor functions were rapidly deteriorating, Boss Nakamura still managed to insert the syringe into a small bottle and fill it with clear liquid. He thumped the needle while watching her ass swing to the beat, becoming more intoxicated by the second. Nakamura stood up on his weary legs and began a slow stagger towards his dancing vixen.

"He's on the move. The serum is taking effect."
With the needle poised between the fingers of his left hand, Boss Nakamura reached for Lexi with his shaky right.

"Now, Jinx!"

Never missing a beat, Lexi whipped around and grabbed his left hand in her right. After twisting it at the wrist, she used her free hand to snatch the syringe from his fingers, and after spinning it in her palm, plunged it into his chest. The sensation of warm liquid filling his heart dropped Boss Nakamura to his knees. As he clutched his chest and gasped for air, Lexi cupped his chin in her right hand and slowly lifted his head.

"Burn in hell, you sick son of a bitch," she whispered while staring into his eyes and smiling.

"Who are you?"

"My friends call me Jinx," she whispered before gripping the crown of his head with her left hand and violently twisting. "Ko, I felt his neck snap in my hands. Does that mean…?"

"Yeah, he's dead," Ko replied after the lifeless body slumped to the floor. "Clear the room and make it to the balcony. Your ride will be waiting."

As Lexi began clearing the room, Ko pulled a grappling gun with a three-pronged hook from his duffle bag. After attaching a cable to the hook, he aimed and fired. Seconds later, the high-speed projectile was embedded in the wall next to the balcony door. Ko then attached a motorized pulley with a harness attached to it and sent across the cable. After donning a gray over coat, Lexi walked out onto the balcony, grabbed the harness, and buckled it around her waist. She stepped over the rail and waited for Ko to release his end of the cable.

"Okay, ride it down to the ninetieth floor. The pickup crew is waiting for you."

After taking a deep breath, Lexi stepped off the ledge and began her rapid decent down the side of the building. While riding the cable, she watched her wig and one of her heels sail off into the night breeze. When she reached the other balcony, two black-clad men, caught her, lifted her over the rail and helped her out of the harness.

"Loved the wig," he said while looking over the side of the building and breathing a sigh of relief.

"I wish I could have kept it," she replied while breathing her own sigh of relief. "Were you nervous?"

"What do you think?" he asked while watching the activities across the street. "I guess you really are bad luck to men."

"Not to you, baby," she whispered while slipping into a slinky, black cocktail dress.

Meanwhile in the penthouse, eight men including a half-naked Ryugi were standing over Boss Nakamura's dead body. Frustrated and frantic, they searched the room for signs of the mysterious woman who had disappeared into thin air.

"We'd better pack it up, folks. The natives just became very restless."

Meanwhile in Denver, Alex was sitting at a quaint sidewalk café dressed in black Dolce & Gabbana slacks, black square-toed Fratelli Rossetti gators, and a cream-colored Hugo Boss shirt. With his legs crossed and his head slightly tilted, he pretended to read the menu. In actuality, Alex was studying a pair of olive-skinned gentlemen seated a few tables from him. Using the facial recognition software in his x-ray equipped glasses, he studied the small-caliber, Walther P99s holstered under each man's left arm while their vital statistics scrolled before his eyes. Within seconds, Alex had their names, height, weight, aliases, places and dates of birth, and a list of crimes committed. Last and certainly most interesting, a bounty for each of them appeared. The turban-wearing man on the left was only worth two hundred-fifty thousand dollars.

Hardly worth the effort, Alex thought while shaking his head.

The balding Armenian on the right in the navy-blue, Perry Ellis three-piece with matching Bacco Bucci leather boots, however, commanded a much higher bounty.

One-million-two-hundred-fifty thousand, he thought while grinning. *That's more like it.*
"Excuse me, sir? Is this seat taken?"

Alex lowered his blue-tinted glasses to the tip of his nose and found himself instantly mesmerized by the stunning, bronze-colored goddess standing at the opposite side of his table. This tall, statuesque beauty and the soft scent of her floral perfume was so intoxicating that he was at a loss for words.

"I don't mean to bother you, but there's nowhere else to sit. Do you mind if I join you?" she asked nervously.

"By all means have a seat," he replied while standing and motioning to the padded wrought iron chair opposite him. "This place does get crowded from time to time."

His warm smile and gentlemanly charm quickly calmed her nerves. She appeared to be moving in slow motion when she sat down and crossed her long, bare, curvaceous legs. Auburn-streaked spirals hung just below her shoulders and her navy-blue, Michael Kors business-suit clung closely to and accentuated her slender, yet well-rounded figure. Her white, low-cut silk blouse gave way to a butter-fly pendant that lay nestled between her bronze melons. Feeling his stares, she playfully used her right hand to brush her hair behind her ear.

Damn! Alex thought to himself while trying not to stare at the lace bra and panties underneath her suit.

"I'm Lynn," she said answering the question he had forgotten to ask. "Do you have a name?"

"I'm sure I do, but it escapes me at the moment."

She looked up from her menu at Alex and quickly noticed his wandering eyes. Though he was maintaining a visual on his marks, Alex found himself becoming more and more distracted by the moment. With her manicured eyebrows slightly raised and a smile on her glossy lips, Lynn quickly appraised the handsome gentleman across the table from her. She could smell his cologne on the breeze. His hair was pulled back in a ponytail, and was the smoothest and blackest she had ever seen, especially on a man. His dark-caramel skin was immaculate, his beard perfectly trimmed. His baritone voice was as smooth as melted chocolate. *This brotha is fine!* she thought to herself.

"So," Lynn began after gathering her wayward thoughts, "you don't know your own name?"

"It's Alexis," he replied after a brief pause. "Alexis Stratton, but you can call me Alex."

"Pleased to meet you, Alex," she replied as her extended hand made its way across the table.

"The pleasure is all mine," he replied before taking it and kissing it softly. "Please excuse me if I seem forward, but you are truly breathtaking. I mean…I've seen beautiful women before, but none of them compare to you. Are you a model? Are you in town for a photo shoot or something?"

"Thank you, but no," she replied after being caught off guard by the familiar yet silky delivery.

The look in his bedroom eyes made her cheeks red and her skin hot. Their mutual gaze continued until she slowly withdrew her hand from his.

"How long have you been in Denver?"

"What makes you think I'm not from here?" she asked curiously.

"I've been in Denver most of my life, so trust me when I say that I'd remember someone as stunning as you."

"You've got me," Lynn replied, trying not to melt before his eyes. *This brotha is good,* she thought while holding her glass and watching him fill it with water.

She hoped he had not noticed that her breasts had swollen or that her hardened nipples were poking against her blazer.

"I'm here from Cincinnati, Ohio, on business."

"How long are you planning on staying? I mean, I was hoping that I could see you again before you left."

"I'd like that, Alex. So, what do you recommend?"

"You mean off the menu?"

"If I didn't know better, Alex, I'd think you were flirting with me."

"Is it that obvious?" he inquired while watching the movements over her shoulder.

"Yes, and I think it's *so* sweet," she replied before the tingling sensation at the base of her spine crept between her tightly clinched thighs.

Sweet did not describe what Alex was doing. His demeanor was downright seductive. Their flirtatious banter continued over grilled chicken salads and warm-buttered bread. Though an hour had passed and Alex's attention was firmly fixed on Lynn, he never lost sight of the two men who had originally caught his eye.

"What do you do in Cincinnati?"

"I'm in nursing school," she replied after dabbing the corners of her mouth. "I hope to become a doctor which is part of the reason I'm in Denver."

"You're here to study medicine?"

"No, I'm here to settle my father's estate. I'm hoping to use the money he left my sister and me to pay for my education," she sighed after her jovial mood suddenly became very somber.

"Sorry to hear about your father's passing."

"Me too, but he's in a better place. His suffering is over."

"Touché," Alex replied after searching for something else to say. "If I ever get sick in Cincinnati, I'll be sure to look you up, Dr. Turner."

"You'd better," she replied, her radiant smile returning as quickly as it left. "Do you have the time, Alex?"

"It is two-forty five," he replied after looking at his Diamond encrusted Bulgari.

"Oh shit! I'm supposed to have an appointment at Weltman, Reid, and Myers at three o'clock. There's no way I'll make it in time."

"Relax," he replied calmly while reaching for his phone. "Dave Weltman is a personal friend of mine. I'll tell him you're with me. You'll be fine."

"You really are a knight in shining armor, Alex Stratton," she declared after breathing a sigh of relief. "Allow me to treat you to lunch at least." "Some other time," he replied with a smile while motioning for the maître de.

Lynn watched as they entered into a brief, but quiet exchange. She stared curiously when he leaned in close and Alex whispered in his ear. After quickly glancing at Lynn, the maître de nodded to Alex and left the table.

"I told him to charge it to the house," he said after lifting his glass and sipping, answering the question she was silently asking.
"The house?"
"Yes, I own this café," he replied nonchalantly.
"I have to go to the bathroom," she said after shaking her head and smiling.
"I'll be here waiting," he smiled before standing and watching her leave.

Once Lynn was out of sight, Alex picked his cell phone up off the table and began scrolling through its phonebook. After making a selection, he pressed *send*.

"Dave Weltman's office. This is Pam speaking."
"Hello, Pam, this is Alexis Stratton. Please inform Mr. Weltman that I am en route with his 3PM appointment."
"Will do, Mr. Stratton."
"Thank you Pam."

After disconnecting the call, Alex immediately began pecking at the phone's virtual keyboard.

"File number 46723942 acquired. BM."
"Where? Delilah."
"Denver. BM"

P D Baldwin

"When? Delilah"
"Now. BM."

After placing the phone back in its case, Alex got up from the table, and walked over to the serving stand where he was greeted by the same maître de. After draping a towel over Alex's left forearm and handing him a pitcher of ice water, he watched Alex walk over to the table where the two marks were seated.

"More water, sir?" Alex inquired to the balding Armenian who arrogantly held his out glass. "For you, sir?"

Not to Alex's surprise, he was completely ignored by his turban-clad table mate. After the balding man took a healthy drink of water, Alex returned to the stand and dumped the pitcher into a nearby drain. As a busboy passed, Alex placed it in his tub of dirty dishes. When Lynn emerged from the café, Alex gently took her by the hand and led her to the curbside where his charcoal-gray, Aston Martin DBS was waiting. Holding the door open as she climbed in, Alex peered over his shoulder to check on his target. Much to his delight his mark was clutching his heart and slowly turning blue. When the coupe pulled away, the man collapsed to the ground taking the entire table with him. Minutes later, the DBS's V-12 purred to a stop in front of a brick high-rise with Weltman, Reid, and Meyers on the marquee.

"So, I'll pick you up at your hotel at seven, right?"
"Yes," Lynn replied with her beautiful smile beaming like the sun. "Thank you for lunch, the ride, everything, Alex."
"It was my pleasure."
"See you later, Alex," she cooed.

He fought the urge to pucker his lips when she leaned over and caressed his stubble covered cheek while staring deeply into his eyes. The sound of her voice and the touch of her hand had Alex's dick twitching in his pants. The mere fact that he had just killed a man had completely escaped his mind. He watched her every movement as she exited the coupe. Feeling his stares on her hips and ass, Lynn put a sensual swing in them before disappearing through the building's smoked glass entry. Just as the door closed, Alex felt a buzz on his hip. He pulled out his cell phone and read the message.

"Kill confirmed. Delilah."

North of Denver, in the city of Boulder Colorado sits an exclusive gated community called Whitman Estates. This subdivision is filled with luxurious homes that have professionally manicured lawns, sprawling landscapes, and are priced from five hundred-thousand to five-million dollars. The neighborhood with its quiet streets and walking trails is far removed from the hustle and bustle of Denver, and in this community, live some of Colorado's most elite citizens.

At the end of a cul-de-sac on a street aptly named Aspiration Lane, sits the largest and most expansive plot in the community. On this ten-acre, tree-lined property is a massive ivory manor-house, which was modeled after a civil war-era Victorian mansion with a pair wrap around porches; one on the first level and one on the second. A large Jamaican flag hung from the second floor balcony flapping proudly in the cool spring breeze. In front of the house is an ivory birdbath in the center of a plush green island a circular, cobblestone driveway with four vehicles parked on it: two white Range Rover Sports, a white S 550 Mercedes sedan, and a candy-apple red Porsche 911, all of which were adorned with Jamaican flag-styled vanity plates. In the rear of the house was a miniature soccer field, a basketball court-sized patio with two wet bars, a pair of hibachi grills, and an Olympic-sized swimming pool that was flanked by a pair of Jacuzzis. In the grass just off the patio were four tables with large white umbrellas, and beyond the tree-lined rear, was a helipad. Patrolling these lavish grounds was a team of armed sentries and Rottweilers on leashes.

On the mansion's second floor overlooking the patio was the master suite, and inside atop the covers of a massive California king, Tisha was pinned beneath a humping, grunting, dark-skinned man. With her legs spread wide and her mind wandering, she lay there in total disgust. Meanwhile, there he was perched between her thighs and sweating like a mad man. When he buried his bald head in the pillow near her neck, she gazed out of the patio doors to her right and prayed silently that he would cum so that this madness could end. To escape this sexual degradation, Tisha tried to imagine he was Alex, but it was no use. He was nowhere near the suave, sexy, and sensual lover she had left just hours ago.

"Mi a cum now, gal!" he proclaimed when he raised his sweat-covered head.
Thank God, she thought while scowling at him.
"Oh, *shit*!" he cried repeatedly with his body quivering and shaking until his dick went limp inside her.

Tisha tried desperately not to dry heave when she felt his bursts, which in her mind were akin to being pissed on, or in this case pissed in. Proud of his performance and grinning like the Joker, he rolled off her to the opposite side of the bed and reached into the top drawer of his nightstand. Now free of his bondage, Tisha clutched the sheets to her neck and quickly turned her back to him. Lying there in disgust and pretending to fall asleep, she was suddenly gagged by the pungent odor of marijuana. When she opened her eyes there was a thick cloud of smoke hovering over the bed. When he started coughing and hacking, she secretly hoped he would choke to death from the smoke he was blowing so liberally in the air.

"Wan some ganja, gal?"
"No thank you, honey."
"Wa mek?" he asked, partially insulted by her refusal.
"I'm just not in the mood now, daddy. That's all."

"Mi a know, gal," he replied before taking a long hit. "Mi a true grindsman!"
"Yes baby, you certainly are," she replied while choking back tears. "Your dick is always too good for me, daddy."

Though his hacking and coughing were sickening by themselves, it was his sadistic laughter that hurt the most. Moments later, silence fell on his side of the bed. Tisha turned over and saw that he had fallen asleep with his hand on his chest and the smoking cigar still between his fingers. She carefully removed it and took a long hit. With smoke in her cheeks and tears in her eyes, she contemplated putting it out on his pitted face. Sadness coursed through her when she stared at him then looked around the bedroom. After taking another hit, Tisha snuffed the cigar out in the ashtray on the black-marble nightstand. Attempting not to disturb the snoring "sex machine," she gently stepped out of the bed and grabbed her robe and her cell.

She walked out the French doors onto the porch and looked out on the trappings of her lifestyle: money, cars, clothes, jewelry, servants, and of course the armed guards. She was a modern day celebrity and had everything a twenty-two year old sista could ever want. She turned around and looked at him once again. Her sobs became so loud that the guards below stopped and began staring up at her. When they began whispering amongst themselves, Tisha backed slowly away from the rail. Her legs gave way when her back found the wall, and she slid down it until she was sitting on the floor with her knees drawn to her chest. After pulling herself together, she pulled her phone out of her pocket and began to dial.

"Hello. Tisha? Is that you?"
"Yes, Dawn, it's me," she sobbed.
"Girl, why are you crying?"
"You know why, Dawn. I hate him."
"Who girl, Simon?"
"Yes, Dawn. Simon."

"Girl, don't trip. You got a good man. So what the dick ain't no good? Every marriage has a flaw, right? Some men don't work. Some men are drunks and some are even junkies. Your man can't fuck. So, what?"

"So, what? Are you serious, Dawn? You think it's just the sex?"

"My bad girl…damn. Does he still hit you?"

"Yes," Tisha replied while trying valiantly to maintain her composure.

"Oh. Well girl, you know some men have a problem expressing how they feel and sometimes a nigga might put his hands on you."

"I don't believe you, Dawn. That nigga put me in the hospital three months ago. Roger has never hit you."

"'Cause he knows I'd kill his ass," she snapped before realizing how insensitive she had been. "Okay, so the nigga got a little physical with you. You know how them Jamaicans are, and what did you expect anyway? You got fly with him in front of his peeps, right?"

"Alex has never hit me, not once. He treats me like a lady all the time and makes love to me like I'm something sent from Heaven."

"You ain't thinking of leaving Simon for Alex again, are you? I mean don't get me wrong. That is a fine, car'mel-colored nigga with a body! Oh my gawd he has a body! And yeah, he owns a few businesses, some cars, and has some dough, but girl, please. Simon is rich! He could buy Alex and ten more niggas just like him. Are you insane?"

"You're right, Dawn. Guys like Simon don't come along very often."

"Tisha, gal, weh yu?"

"Your brother-in-law is beckoning so I have to go."

"Make the best of it, Tish. Call me later."

"Bye, Dawn."

Tisha quickly disconnected the phone call and proceeded to fix her face as best she could. When she returned to the room, Simon was lying there in bed with the covers turned back. He was stroking his dick while puffing on his cigar.

"Come now, mi hose need some lovin."

Recalling her pep talk, Tisha crawled back into the bed next to him and closed her eyes before moving in to kiss his cheek. The pain of her hair being yanked and her head being snapped back made her eyes open wide with horror.

"Mi nuh wan no kiss, woman!" he barked while shoving her head towards his dick.

There was nothing sensual about the way he gripped the back of her head. Clearly, he was not the tender lover that Alex was. He taunted her and grunted while aggressively thrusting his dick in and out of her mouth. Tisha contemplated biting him, but flashed back to the severe beating she took the last time she did and decided against it. With tears in her eyes, she endured it like she had so many times in the past. A primal roar escaped his thin blackened body before he released his load into her mouth. He held her head in place while his thick white paste coated her throat and gagged. Tisha dry-heaved several times on the way to the master bath before puking into the cold porcelain toilet. While crying and vomiting, she heard him laughing from the bedroom.

"Yu hab da hang of dat one day, chile."

For the rest of this story, read the upcoming book *Operation Cover-up: Rise of the Black Mamba* by P D Baldwin.